AN INVITATION TO TEA

A HISTORICAL ROMANCE NOVELLA

JESSICA BAKER

First edition: June 2021.

ISBN: 978-1-7347202-5-9 (paperback).
ISBN: 978-1-7347202-4-2 (e-book).

Published 2021 by Celestial Pen Books.

A NOTE TO THE READERS

Dear Readers,

While this story is set in the same universe as the books in *A Lady Thea Mystery* series, this is not a mystery.

It takes place two years before the events in *Murder on the Flying Scotsman*, but it is not necessary to read any of the Lady Thea's mysteries in order to enjoy this book.

If you enjoy this book, please consider leaving a review.

This book has been edited and proofread. However, authors and editors are not infallible, so if you find errors, please contact me at the social media links below or contact@jessicabakerauthor.com.

Thank you.

THE CRAVEN FAMILY

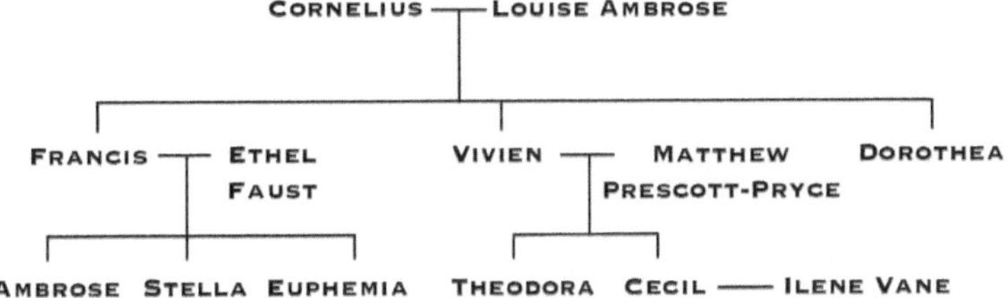

1

———

STELLA

LONDON - JUNE 1908

IF EXCITEMENT WAS TANGIBLE, the air around Stella Craven might have crackled with it. For the first time since she came to London, she could pretend that she was just there for an adventure and a bit of fun. Today she wouldn't worry about marriage or about any of her other troubles. Today, she was a bird with a full set of feathers on her wings.

Before she finally agreed to the outing, her mother spent an hour ranting about the Exhibition and its crowds. Mrs. Craven came to chaperone, walking a few paces behind Stella. Her disapproving comments could barely be heard over the roar of the people.

Stella had only one goal in mind that morning when she decided to brave the bustling crowds and venture into the Franco-British Exhibition. She was there to get chocolate, as many Menier Chocolates as she could possibly carry. It also served to help her forget her anticipation for Cal's response to her letter.

"Honestly, darling," her mother complained as she trailed behind. "Wouldn't you rather be inside somewhere? A museum, perhaps?"

"The museums will still be here next year."

The atmosphere was glorious. The warmth of the summer sun smiled down upon them, a rare reprieve from the gloomy, stormy London days she had yet to grow used to. Stella wanted to spin, to fling her arms wide and laugh loudly. She didn't, though. Her mother might have a heart attack if she did.

"We're almost there, Mother. It's so pleasant out today." At her mother's scoff, Stella glanced back to see the older woman hiding under her parasol. Her mother dabbed obsessively with a lace handkerchief at the sweat that beaded on her forehead.

"I don't understand why you so desperately need chocolate."

"Chocolate is one of life's few pleasures."

"I do believe that's what you say about clothing."

"Fashion, Mother, not clothing," Stella all but spat the last word. "*Couture* fashion, not Prêt-à-Porter, are works of art and far more exciting than any museum."

"A museum is more lasting. You shop for new clothes every six months."

So did every other debutante and aristocratic matron. No one wanted to be on the front of the society pages in last year's dress.

Stella pouted. "You want me to look fashionable and make an impression in society. Didn't you hear Mrs. Vanderbilt's comment about my dress when we were in Newport? She said that I was ahead of the trends."

She had stepped into the first ball at their Newport home wearing a crimson Delphos gown that clung to her body, making her resemble a Grecian statue. For Stella, there had been a certain amount of pleasure derived from the look on her mother's face when she emerged from the throngs of their Worth-clad society friends.

"That's because she didn't know how else to tactfully tell you that your outfit was ridiculous."

"Stylish." Her eyes caught the wide, squared archway with the name "Chocolat-Menier" declared in tall letters. Stella resisted the urge to point and race forward. Before she entered society, she might have gotten away with it. Her mother would never put up with it now. "There."

Display cases on each side highlighted the elaborate showcase of their goods, as well as some of the awards Menier Chocolate had won. Miniature cases wrapped around the inside. She couldn't wait to study each one.

Stella clasped her hands together to stop herself from rushing inside. Childish delight took over as she saw a dozen souvenirs positioned near the exits. As she reached for one of the postcards with the arch, she was met by a glare from the older Craven woman. "Haven't we spent enough time here?"

A glance at her watch told her they'd barely been at the Exhibition for thirty minutes. Most of that time had been spent walking.

She closed her eyes and took a deep breath. She knew they wouldn't spend the whole day there. It was too much to expect her mother to allow her to stay long, despite this being a once-in-a-lifetime opportunity. Stella wanted to see everything else that was there, but it was better to appease her mother now and come back later without her. Despite the act she put on for the rest of the world, Ethel Faust Craven was the kind of mother who cared very little about her family's happiness.

"Yes, Mother," she said, barely keeping the bite from her words. A sour feeling turned her gut. She collected herself and followed her mother out of the exhibit.

"MISS," her maid, Jeanette, said in lieu of a greeting when they came back to their suite. "A letter came for you while you were out."

"A letter?" Her heart raced at the thought, and she ignored her maid's disapproving glare. *Cal.*

"I put it in your room."

Stella nodded. A thrill rushed through her as she raced into the other room, the chocolates all but forgotten on the coffee table.

THE LETTER SAT in Stella's hands like a weight. The outside envelope had the Countess of Wraughtley written in dark, swirling letters on thick parchment. Why would the Countess write to her? For the life of her, Stella couldn't remember meeting this particular countess. But then again, she had met so many people in the last month—an endless parade of people she'd likely never see again—that she could hardly remember all of them.

She flipped it over, examining the green wax seal. The crest was a raised fox ready to strike. Stella picked up a letter opener and slid it through the opening on the side. The paper ripped apart with a soft sound, leaving frayed edges behind.

The Countess' letter matched the penmanship from the outside envelope. Each curl and loop made Stella wish she had paid more attention to such things in school. The letter looked like a piece of art and showcased the woman's status.

"Dear Miss Craven," it began, followed by words that made Stella want to crumple the paper and throw it into the fireplace. She took a deep breath.

According to the Countess, Stella had agreed to take tea with the woman and her son—two people she had never even met—in a letter she never wrote. Why would she have agreed to such a thing? She didn't want to meet the woman, and she certainly didn't want to meet her son.

All she wanted was to go home. To go back to the States,

back to Chicago. To be allowed to marry who she wished. To be able to live her life as she desired. She knew she would have to marry, but she wanted a say in who he would be. If her mother had her way, she wouldn't.

Other girls from her school always giggled over the idea of marrying a great lord in England or a Rockefeller or an Astor or a Vanderbilt. Stella never told them that she would have happily given up her furs and silks and jewels to marry into the middle class if it got her free of her mother's grasp.

Her mother wanted her to have a title and to be accepted into society completely. Countess or lady or whatever the son's wife's title would be probably sounded perfect to her mother. Her mother's only claim to society had been her family's new money. That wasn't good enough for anyone in America. However, in England, a title could practically be purchased if you had the money to pay for it.

Stella gathered up her skirt and marched into the sitting room.

"I'm not going, Mother."

Her mother sat on the sofa, the picture of innocence, reading the newspaper. A flowered tea service sat on the table before her, her cup filled to the brim. A second cup sat upside-down on the saucer. She had obviously ordered it in the hope that Stella would join her for tea, but after this, Stella hardly wanted to be near her.

At Stella's words, she lowered the paper slowly. Stella thought her mother seemed to be inconvenienced by her daughter interrupting her reading.

"What are you talking about?"

Stella held up the letter. "Lady Wraughtley wrote to me. She thanked me for my kind letter." With that, she brought it up to her face, reading off the page. "'I am delighted to hear that you and your mother will be joining Lord Pemberton and me for tea.'" She dropped the letter and the envelope on the table. If she thought she could get away with slamming it down, she would have. "I never wrote her a letter."

Her mother picked it up and examined the page the same way she would jewelry.

Undeterred, Stella pushed on. "Therefore, it'd be horribly rude for me to meet them under false pretenses since I'm not the one who accepted the Countess' invitation."

Her mother patted the spot next to her on the sofa in a clear invitation for Stella to sit. In reality, she knew it wasn't a suggestion. Her mother didn't want to stand, and she didn't like Stella towering over her. It was about power and her mother keeping control.

Stella wasn't ready to give in all the way, though, and chose the chair across the table instead. If she sat next to her mother, the older woman would wrap her arm around her shoulders and say something to make Stella feel guilty. Perhaps guilty enough to agree to almost anything. It would be easier to stand her ground if she kept her distance.

"It was very kind of the Countess to extend her offer in the first place," her mother said neutrally. Her face gave away nothing.

She held out the letter to Stella. When Stella didn't take it, she set it down on the table as though it was something to be treasured.

Stella clenched her fists. Her nails dug into her palm. "So you did write to her." Her mother stayed silent. "Mother, why?"

"It is just an invitation for tea," the older woman said dismissively. "It is hardly a marriage proposal."

Stella scowled as she reached for the envelope and picked at the sealing wax bearing the Wraughtley crest. The fox seemed to laugh at her.

"Wraughtley," she spat out as her finger traced the letters

of the word. "Even their name sounds dreadful. Like something's dying."

Her mother sighed exasperatedly, but Stella didn't look up at her. She knew from past experience that this was where her mother would resort to more outright demands.

"Please do not say that at tea." Her mother took her newspaper, shook out the wrinkles that had appeared while it had lain in her lap, and lifted it back to her face.

"Perhaps I should tell them. I'm sure none of those stuffy British girls have."

Her mother folded the newspaper and laid it beside her on the sofa. She glared at Stella, but Stella continued on despite that.

"They're all too busy batting their eyes and giggling to give their honest opinion about anything."

"Stella," her mother warned.

But Stella had stepped onto her soapbox, and she wasn't climbing back down. Instead, she moved to the window. Outside, people strolled down the street two-by-two. If she didn't know better, she'd say it was the only way they knew how to walk.

"That's all they care about: marriage and titles and how big their castle is." She shook her head, closing her eyes as she did so. "I don't understand it."

"Stella!" her mother snapped, and Stella whipped back to look at her. Her mother was on her feet, eyes blazing. "Do not say those things to the Countess or her son. How you act is a reflection upon me."

Stella crossed her arms. She dug her fingernails into her sleeves until she was sure she was cutting the skin underneath.

"Then why don't you just send me home? I'd much rather be home in Chicago than here shopping for a marriage."

Her mother would never do that. Her mother couldn't control Stella as easily in Chicago. Stella had friends. She had

Calvin Wright—Cal—who had promised to marry her and save her from her family's expectations. He would be her freedom. She wouldn't be forced into some ruse of a marriage to a lord who would care nothing for her.

"You will be on your best behavior for the Countess and her son."

Stella turned back to the window. The sight of her mother made her want to cry. To scream. To take that teacup off the table and fling it into the fireplace.

Behind her, she heard her mother sit back down. Glass clinked softly in a telltale rattle as her mother set the cup and saucer down on the table.

"Can you not see I am only trying to help you? You will need allies here."

Stella swallowed a sob. "You make it sound like I am going to war."

"Marriage is war, darling." Her mother sighed. "I am trying to give you a future."

Stella fought the urge to snort. *Like she actually cared.* She just wanted a titled daughter to tell the world about.

Look at how I succeeded with my daughter, she could almost hear her mother say to those women in Chicago who doubted them because her mother had been from new money. *Without breeding and status, I still managed to sell my daughter off to the most noble title.*

The cup clinked again. The newspaper rustled. Stella refused to look at the woman on the sofa.

"Fine, Mother," she said softly, admitting her defeat in a battle that she would never win. "I won't say a word." Stella took a deep breath and composed herself. She didn't want to leave her mother having the last word. That would be too close to actually letting her mother beat her into submission. "I would hate to be an embarrassment to you."

With that, Stella turned and stormed from the room, unable to stand being in the same place as her mother. She closed the door to her bedroom quietly, although she would have liked to slam it shut. Angrily, she tore the pins from her hair and unbuttoned her shirt. She couldn't breathe, but not having the starched, ruffled collar running up her throat helped.

She collapsed in the chair beside her bed, as much as she could collapse in her corset, and buried her face into her hands. She wanted to cry, but she would not. She could not let her mother win.

Outside, the skies opened up, and it started to rain.

2

———————

WILLIAM

THE CAB BOUNCED down the street, hitting potholes and ruts, but William Pemberton wouldn't have been in a better mood even if it had been the smoothest ride he ever had. It would have taken a miracle to make him feel better after his awful day. His stomach turned as they hit yet another hole, and he clenched his fingers tighter around the handle of the briefcase.

After what felt like a lifetime, the driver slowed, and they stopped in front of the marbled front of Wraughtley Place. The rain slowed to a drizzle, but the water had puddled on the sidewalk.

William gathered up his briefcase and stepped down from the cab. He paid the driver what he owed the man, climbed the rain-slicked stairs of the townhouse, and pushed the door open.

"Mother?" he called to the empty foyer. The curtains were drawn, but the lights were not yet lit. If he didn't know better, he would say no one was home. "Where are you?"

In the corner, a shadowed figure fidgeted, shifting foot to foot. A white-frilled hat caught the light.

"Have you seen the Countess?" he asked the maid, a girl probably half his age that he didn't entirely recognize. The girl turned. Her cheeks burned red even in the dimness of the hall. She dipped into a shallow curtsy and kept her eyes turned downwards.

"She's upstairs, milord. In the study."

He nodded and took the stairs two at a time until he reached the first floor. He pushed the door to the study open and stepped inside.

The room was bare. All of his great-grandmother's knick-knacks and trinkets that lined the shelves when he was a child had been sold off for whatever meager sum they could fetch. Any of the paintings and books that were worth something had been auctioned off. The sun-faded imprints that pockmarked the wallpaper were all that remained of them.

His mother was working intently on a letter at the desk by the window, a smile on her face. He was glad to see she had a better day than he did. When she heard him, she glanced up at him.

"There you are, darling. I just received word from the Cravens about tea tomorrow."

The Cravens? He vaguely remembered her talking about going to tea with them, but he hadn't been paying much attention. He had been too worried about the meeting with the loan officer. And she was going on about tea.

"That is not important right now, Mother." William collapsed onto the sofa and peeled his glasses from his face. He ran his hands over his face, trying to rid himself of the pinch in his nose. He set his glasses on the table. He hated how tired they made his eyes. "I just returned from the bank. They have denied our loan."

He could hear her gently set the pen on the table.

"Pem…"

He hated that name. He'd been stuck with it since childhood when he couldn't pronounce his own last name correctly. And then it had become his title, and then everyone began to call him it.

"It's no use, is it?" he asked her, but he refused to look up from his hands. "We're going to lose everything."

His mother exhaled softly. Her chair creaked.

"We have to tell Father. He thinks money is just a bit tight. He has no idea—"

The sofa shifted beside him as she sat down. He looked up at her. "All hope is not lost. The Cravens have money. If you were to marry, you would have access to her inheritance—"

He was on his feet before he could think too much about it, and the words fell from his mouth without his permission, "They'd need to own the Bank of Bloody England for it to do any good!"

His mother clutched at her chest, her eyes wide.

"William Pemberton!"

The anger he felt didn't die down. It still simmered under the surface, ready to reappear at a moment's notice.

"I'm sorry, Mother."

His mother didn't deserve his rage. It wasn't her fault that they were going bankrupt. Too many generations spent away their savings without doing anything to bring money in. Even his mother had not been the heiress that the family needed. Her family owned a small estate north, but she had only been a baron's daughter.

He shook his head, reached for his glasses, and put them back on. He glanced around the room. As a child, it was one of his favorite places in Wraughtley Place. Now, it was just a painful reminder of how much they already lost. If this continued, they would lose everything.

"I feel so helpless. Our tenants depend on us. The land has been in our family for generations."

And if he didn't do anything… if he didn't find a solution…

The prospect made him lightheaded. He gripped the arm of the sofa, trying his best to regain his balance.

"The problems existed long before you were born."

Her words weren't the reassurance he was looking for. His mother rose from the sofa, as graceful as ever, and he straightened.

"Why did no one do anything about them?"

His mother patted his shoulder and rubbed a comforting hand over his back. William turned his head slightly to give her a small smile, but he feared it was more of a grimace.

"You'll figure out what to do, Pemmy."

She squeezed his shoulder and glided from the room. Her skirts swept the floor behind her. He stared after her, waiting until the door closed behind her before he sank back down the sofa.

Perhaps he could get another appointment with the bank. Maybe he could find someone who would be willing to help him. Anything would be better than Mother's tea party, wasting time with some girl who would only want him for his title.

Was his mother really hoping to marry him off to some girl to save what was left of their estate? It wasn't as if it was unheard of. All those American girls came with fortunes. How the inheritances were distributed was different in America than in England. Many of the daughters received an equal share of the family's wealth over there. Perhaps Miss Craven was no different, an heiress to a financier or a railroad or an oil company.

William let out a breath and stood, moving to the desk to unpack his briefcase. He could stand to look over the ledgers again. He would see if someone at the bank was available to meet him first thing in the morning. This time, he would be more prepared for whatever they threw at him.

3

——————

STELLA

STELLA STARED out the window of her hotel room, watching off into the distance. The rain had cleared, and from her bed, she could see the smoke climbing from the tops of buildings. She felt like a child locked in her bedroom as punishment rather than by choice.

"The Importance of the Vote," the speech that Mrs. Pankhurst had given only months ago, sat open on her lap, but she couldn't focus on reading it. How could she? As women were getting closer to finally winning everything she had ever desired, Stella was preparing to be sold like chattel to whoever had the best title. At this point, it seemed Lord Pemberton would be that person.

The idea that she would have no choice in a husband made her gut turn. If it had been up to her, she would marry Cal. Her mother would never approve of the match, though. As an American law student with no real money, title, or influence to his name, her lifelong friend, Calvin Wright was persona non grata in her mother's book. Not that Stella cared about Cal as more than a friend, but he was the best of all her bad options. The idea of deciding who she would spend the rest of her life with at twenty-one, when she had yet to experience life, seemed silly. But her mother was insistent, and there was no arguing with her mother.

The doors rattled as someone tried to turn the handle, only to find it locked. They knocked, and Stella looked up.

"Miss Stella!" her maid, Jeanette, called from the other side of the door as she knocked again. Her voice was pleading, and Stella knew that the maid would raise a fuss if she couldn't get in. She might even go to her mother's maid, Blakely, who would involve her mother. Then Stella would be in more trouble than she already was. "Please unlock the door."

Stella closed her eyes and tucked the pamphlet beneath the pillow before she stood and strode to the door. She paused a moment, took a deep breath, and then she unlocked the door and pulled it open.

In the sitting room, Jeanette stood posed with her hand raised.

Stella walked back to the bed and sat on the edge, waiting for her maid to tell her why she was interrupting her sulking. Stella didn't dare call it anything but that. She knew she was acting childish, but she felt, in this case, she was a bit justified.

Jeanette dropped her hand and walked into the room.

"Miss Stella, your mother sent me to help you select a dress for you to wear tomorrow."

Jeanette switched the lights on. The burst of brightness from the electricity surprised Stella despite expecting it. The maid moved over to the wardrobe and threw the doors open. She pushed through the dresses that she had unpacked and hung with care. They had only just been bought in Paris before they came to England. Her mother presented them as a bribe for Stella to behave, but she knew better. Her mother always complained about Stella buying such an elaborate wardrobe, but these clothes were just wrapping to display a picture of wealth to potential husbands.

She'd hate them if they weren't so gorgeous.

"Do you think this is fair?" Stella couldn't help but ask.

Jeanette paused her actions to look at Stella. "Miss?"

"This whole situation. I hate this. I hate feeling so helpless."

She dropped her head into her hands. Tears prickled at her eyes. Angrily, she brushed at them, hoping to keep them from falling. She refused to cry. If she did, her mother would win, and she wasn't willing to admit that level of defeat.

"I'm sorry, miss," Jeanette said softly.

"There's nothing that you can do."

She glanced up as Jeanette pulled out a soft white lace gown and presented it for approval. Stella took it between her fingers, stroking the bottom of the dress. She remembered buying it only a few weeks ago. It had been so unlike her, but something about the gown made her smile. It was softer than her usual choices, more feminine and delicate than the suits and bright colors she favored for the day.

"That would be acceptable."

"Mrs. Craven thought so too," her maid told her.

It felt like a bucket of cold water had been poured over her head. The gown slipped from between her fingers and onto the bed. Anything her mother approved of, at the moment, was unacceptable.

She couldn't even trust Jeanette's loyalty these days. Anything Stella did or said would likely be immediately reported to Blakely and onto her mother.

Stella stood, pushing past Jeanette to look through the wardrobe herself. She pulled out a pale green gown with white lace.

"I'll be wearing this tomorrow."

It was as delicate as she was willing to go. She'd pair it with a dark purple hat and gloves and gold accents. The colors the suffragists wore, and her mother knew that. Suffragettes, as they were called in England. Her hatpins perhaps or even the gold locket Cal had given her. Wearing a necklace that another man had given her, that would be a real statement.

Jeanette opened her mouth to protest, but Stella really wasn't in the mood. "If that's all, you can go."

She stared at her maid, daring her to argue. Jeanette bowed her head and pressed her lips together tightly. Her mother would know by dinnertime, she was sure. "Yes, miss."

With that, the maid turned and walked out the door.

Stella resisted the urge to scream. It wouldn't do any good. The only way to deal with her mother was to go along with what the woman said. She would have to find her own way to be free. No one was going to help her with that.

4

WILLIAM

WILLIAM GLANCED out the window of the study as the taxi drove up to the front of the house and parked, waiting for him to come down. He gathered his papers and slid them into his briefcase. He needed to be collected and prepared. He doubted he would get another chance at the loan if this meeting went poorly.

It had been like fate. He was heading downstairs to call the bank again to see about setting up another appointment when he received a call from the loan officer. He told William he was available to meet in an hour. He met with his manager and thought they could work something out.

"Pemmy?" his mother called from behind him. Her voice was filled with confusion. "What on earth are you doing?"

William didn't look at her. He didn't have the time to stop and talk.

"I have a meeting at the bank."

"Now? It's hardly ideal."

He bit back a laugh. His mother didn't comprehend how important this was and never had. She might have understood the pressure he was under if her father had no sons. Her brother sold off a portion of the land and turned a decent profit from it. His mother would never understand why that wasn't an option for Wraughtley, at least not while Father was earl.

William snapped the buckle closed and straightened up, gathering his courage.

"Yes, now. I hope since they called, they might approve the loan."

He paused to smile at his mother before he continued through the door and down the stairs. She followed him, her shoes clicking on each step. She radiated thinly veiled annoyance that only grew the closer he got to the door.

"And what about tea?"

Her hands were not on her hips or crossed defensively over her chest, but they might as well have been. Her eyes were filled with fury, but she would never let it leak into her voice. That would be truly unbecoming.

"I'm sorry, Mother. This is urgent. If I manage to get the loan now, I can finally tell Father some good news." He paused by the door. Mr. Farley, the butler, held William's coat out for William to slide his arms into. His mother stepped forwards and brushed his collar down, straightening his tie. Most would think the gesture to be some sort of peace offering. He knew better. "I'll be late to the tea—"

"Not too late, I hope," she muttered under her breath.

"—room, if I even make it at all."

"It's at Claridge's."

"I'll try my best," he promised, with little intention of making it. It would be rude to let her make excuses to the Cravens, but he hardly wanted yet another marriage interview with a giggling girl whose head was filled with all sorts of romantic notions of being a countess.

He moved past her, rushing out the door and into the waiting taxi.

5

STELLA

THE CLARIDGE WAS A GORGEOUS HOTEL. The tearoom was as beautiful as the rest of the building. Tall square pillars and crystal chandeliers decorated the space. Stella felt like she was in some sort of catalogue. Perhaps one of the postcards that she had seen at the Franco-British Exhibition only days ago. Maybe even a painting.

Fashionable women in their large, feathery hats and lacy, floaty gowns surrounded tables. Most looked like they were barely able to sit in their overtightened corsets and hobble skirts. Stella spotted a few couples staring at each other lovingly and laughing at jokes that only they knew. Teacups clinked against saucers, and the smell of sweet cakes and cucumber sandwiches filled the air.

The maître d' led her mother to a table near the center of the room. Obediently, Stella followed. The man pulled the chairs out for Stella and her mother before he left. As they sat, she caught her mother's gaze. If looks could kill, Stella would have been already buried.

"You couldn't have worn anything else?" her mother had asked in the hotel room when she first saw Stella's choice of outfit. From the looks the other patrons cast at them, the white and green gown with the purple accessories made the exact statement she hoped for.

Stella discreetly pulled off her gloves and tucked them beneath the napkin. She knew how to behave, despite her mother's beliefs. But her mother was right about one thing: Stella was going to war, and she was going to fight with the weapons available to her.

"Please do not talk back to the Countess."

Stella sighed, not even looking up. "Yes, Mother."

She reached into her purse and felt blindly for the envelope. The letter had been downstairs waiting for her when they had reached the lobby. She picked it up while her mother was distracted talking to another woman. Stella hadn't dared take the risk to open it up. But feeling it now was comforting.

"What are you playing with?" her mother asked. Stella jumped. Her hands froze beneath the table. She hoped the panic didn't show on her face.

"Nothing. I'll stop." She pulled her hands out of her lap and glanced at her watch instead before turning towards the door. No one who looked like a countess had come in, not that she had any idea what the Countess looked like. "The Countess is late."

Her mother's eyes narrowed. "We are simply early."

"On time is more like it," she scoffed. Her mother sighed and took her napkin off of the table, unfolding it and setting it in her lap. "Right. I'm sorry, Mother."

She needed to be a good daughter. The perfect daughter. The kind of person who wouldn't have been out of place in a Jane Austen novel.

A woman paused at their table and eyed Stella, hesitating as she saw the colors she was wearing. Her mother stood, and Stella followed suit. She assumed this woman was the Countess they were waiting for. The Countess shook her mother's hand.

"Mrs. Craven, it is lovely to see you again." She cast a disparaging eye over Stella's clothes again before she settled on Stella's face. "And you must be Stella. You have the most beautiful penmanship."

Stella glanced at her mother before she smiled at the woman as sweetly as she could. "Thank you."

The Countess sat, and they followed.

"I am very sorry for being so late. I hope you were not too inconvenienced."

Her mother shook her head, smiling all the while. "We only just arrived ourselves."

Stella fought the urge to roll her eyes. Of course, her mother would say anything to be agreeable. She was incredibly averse to confrontations outside of the family. They were never early. They were never insulted by someone else's insults. And, most of all, they were never inconvenienced by someone else.

With that exaggerated grin on her face, her mother continued. "Countess, if you do not mind me asking, I thought Lord Pemberton was joining us?"

The Countess glanced down. "He was supposed to, but he's always been terrible about keeping track of time. I am sure he is just running late." She was lying. Stella could see it from the way the British woman avoided their eyes. She turned to Stella. "Tell me about yourself."

Stella froze. "I—"

The Countess smiled. Stella dug her nails into the skin on her arm and hoped she didn't draw blood through her sleeve.

"There is no need to be shy," the older woman prodded.

Under the table, her mother's boot hit her shin, and Stella fought the urge to jump.

Oblivious to what was happening, the Countess continued, "Do you like to ride?"

"Not horses, no. I dri—" Stella cut off as her mother glared across the table. She intertwined her fingers and stared at her hands to avoid looking at either woman. She wondered if they noticed.

Of course, driving an automobile or riding a bicycle wouldn't be acceptable for a woman. At least in her mother's eyes anyway. How could it be? It would allow her too much freedom away from chaperones who would rather keep a close eye on her.

"That is a shame," the Countess said as if Stella had never slipped up. "The morning rides through the park are excellent. Well then, do you play?"

"Play?"

"An instrument. You play one, don't you?"

Her mother jumped in before she could speak. "Stella plays the violin. She is very good."

The Countess' brow furrowed. "That is a rather modern choice of instrument."

Her mother nodded, her expression serious. "Her father insisted."

The Countess' disapproval of such a choice was clear. After all, violins were traditionally masculine instruments. Her father's command that she learned to play it had caused some strife in the Craven household.

Fortunately, the waiter approached with a pot of tea and spared Stella from whatever disparaging comment the British woman could come up with. Her mother reached for the pot and served them.

"So what else do you usually do, Stella?"

"I am afraid that I am not all that interesting, Countess." Her heart raced. The room was too loud, and the table was too small. She couldn't stay there and be scrutinized by this woman. Whatever she said would be the wrong answer. She jumped to her feet. "Please excuse me. I need some air."

"Wait—" her mother called, but Stella ignored her as she darted from the table.

Stella took careful steps until she was hidden behind one of the pillars. Away from her mother, it felt like she could breathe again, which only made her feel worse. How terrible of a daughter was she that being away from her mother was such a relief?

She reached into her purse and pulled Cal's envelope out. She slid her finger under the edge of the flap. Why didn't she take a knife from the table to open it?

Inside was a letter from Cal. He missed her. He would buy her a ticket to return to the States with him and his aunt. They would leave at the end of July, after his cousin's wedding. Cal told her how his cousin met someone in England, and as he was escorting his aunt back to America after the wedding, so it would be proper for her to join them.

She sighed in relief. They could live their lives free of their parent's expectations. They could be married, just like they had talked about before he went away to school. It would be a marriage based on friendship, but it was a far better fate than being trapped thousands of miles from home with a man who couldn't even bother to show his face for tea.

She grinned and kissed the letter. The gesture was probably considered vulgar. At the moment, she hardly cared. She was going to be free. "Thank you, Cal."

"And who is Cal?" a low voice came from behind her. She jumped. Her hand clutched at her heart as if she could stop it from beating out of her chest. She thrust the letter behind her back as a man—a blond-haired, brown-eyed man probably not much older than her but otherwise completely unmemorable—stepped around the pillar. His gray suit fit him perfectly, though, and the fabric looked like it would be soft to run her fingers across.

"Why does that matter to you?" she demanded. *Why did she feel so guilty about being caught?* He didn't know her. She sighed and moved to put the letter into her purse. It slipped out of her hands, and the man picked it up and read it. "What are you doing?!"

"So, who is Cal?"

"If you must know, he is my fiancé."

"Oh?" The man smirked at her. "And why is he not here with you? Or why are you not with him?"

"It is a complicated story." Stella reached for the letter, but the man held it out of her reach, above her head, and motioned for her to continue. She let out an exasperated sound, one that if her mother ever heard, she'd skin her alive. "We're not actually engaged. Not yet, anyway."

The marriage was a mutually beneficial arrangement for her and Cal. He got a society wife and her money to help back him in his career. She got a marriage free of the expectations of being the kind of wife her mother expected her to be.

The man raised his brows and stared at her like she was stupid. "That doesn't sound so complicated."

Stella glared at him, recrossing her arms. She all but spat the words when she spoke, "My mother doesn't accept our relationship. She forced me to come here, hoping she could set me up with somebody with a title."

"Is *Cal* not good enough?"

"He's a lawyer, but that's not glamorous enough for Mrs. Astor and the Four Hundred, so it's not glamorous enough for Mother."

Stella peeked around the pillar to the table. The man hovered over her, breathing down her neck. Her mother looked up, and Stella nearly knocked into him as she moved back to hide again.

"I think if my mother has her way, I just met my future mother-in-law."

She closed her eyes.

"In her ideal world, I'd go to the altar without meeting the man she wants me to marry so I wouldn't have a chance to protest."

"I'm sure it's not so bad."

Stella looked at him. The man gave her a small smile, and she glared. It was easy for him to say. He wasn't the one with unreasonable expectations being thrust upon him. She sighed, the fight leaving her body.

"He didn't even show up today. No note or word to let us know that we're wasting our time." She clenched fists tight enough that her nails dug into her palm, leaving tiny red crescents. "Honestly, I can't wait to go home."

Stella ducked her head as she rubbed her eye. A handkerchief appeared in front of her. She glanced at him before taking it and wiping her face. He didn't meet her eyes.

"I am sure the man your mother has picked out doesn't want to be a part of this any more than you do."

"You're probably right." She let out a deep breath. "I'm terribly sorry for telling you all that. It had to be more than you bargained for."

"It was, but not entirely unexpected. You should get back." His voice was surprisingly gentle. He reached into his pocket and checked his watch. "I'm late for an appointment. I should be going."

"Of course." She smiled at him. Despite how the conversation started, it had taken a good turn. It surprised her how reluctant she felt that she was to leave and go back to the table. "Thank you for listening."

He handed her the envelope, and she tucked it into her purse. She needed to be more careful with it. The man stayed behind the pillar as she mentally prepared herself to go back to the table. She took a step forward.

As she moved into view, her mother glared disapprovingly at her. She took measured steps to the table.

"Is everything alright?" her mother asked when she got

closer. Stella paused behind her chair, hesitating. She bowed her head slightly and hoped she looked sufficiently subservient.

"I apologize, Countess. I have no idea what came over me." She forced a smile on her face and prayed neither of the older women saw it was taking everything in her not to let it drop.

"That is quite all right." The Countess smiled warmly. "Your mother was telling me that you went to the Franco-British Exhibition."

That brought a grin to Stella's face. The sights and smells at the Exhibition were divine. It was like a little city filled with several palaces. There were even entire villages of people from Senegal and Ireland.

"I very much enjoyed going to Chocolat-Menier."

The Countess smiled at that before her eyes locked on something, or someone, over Stella's shoulder. "Oh, William! There you are."

Stella looked back. She wondered if her face had paled or if the floor had fallen from beneath her. If she wasn't sitting, she might have fainted as the man from before approached their table.

"You!" she hissed before she could help it. Her mother glared at her even as her boot dug into Stella's ankle. The man, apparently William Pemberton, grinned sheepishly at Stella, clearly embarrassed to be caught in his earlier deception. She scowled. Good. He should be.

"This is my son, Viscount Pemberton," the Countess declared before looking up at her son. "William, this is Mrs. Craven and Miss Stella Craven."

Of course, her mother ignored Stella's look of outrage in favor of turning to the young lord with a smile that said nothing was wrong plastered on her face.

"It's a pleasure, Lord Pemberton. We have heard much about you."

"The pleasure is mine. I apologize for my tardiness. I had some other business to attend to."

Stella fought the snort she wished she could give. Other business. Sure. Harassing random women in tearooms definitely counted as business.

He reached for the empty chair, the one to her left, and sat. A waiter rushed over with a teacup and saucer. Stella laid her hands in her lap, digging her fingers into her palm again.

"That's quite all right," her mother continued. "We're glad you were able to make it." She turned, staring pointedly at Stella before she spoke. "Right, Stella?"

Lord Pemberton smiled at them. It seemed he was pretending she hadn't spilled her guts to him behind that pillar only minutes before. She shrank back in her chair and hoped it would swallow her even as she muttered, "Yes, glad."

The young lord glanced over at her, his smile as insincere as his next words, "I look forward to speaking with you more."

HOW COULD she have been so stupid? She wasn't a child incapable of keeping her mouth shut. And yet, she had gone and told that horrid man everything.

Stella stormed into her room like a woman on a mission. She barely noticed Jeanette hanging the laundry in the wardrobe.

"That man!" she declared, shuddering as she did so. The mere thought of him left a sour taste in her mouth. "He's dreadful. Absolutely horrible!"

Jeanette stayed silent.

"I refuse to stay here a moment longer."

She needed to leave London. She would prefer to leave the country. She wished she could get a ticket, but her mother controlled their purses. Other than a small allowance, Stella had no access to any money.

Would it be enough to settle somewhere else while she waited for Cal? She opened her trunk and pulled clothes from the wardrobe, piling them in as carefully as she could. Jeanette stared at her like Stella was the one who had lost her mind.

"Help me pack. Immediately!"

It was unfortunate that her mother entered the room at that moment. When she spoke, her words could have summoned fire if such a thing were possible. "Lord Pemberton was a perfect gentleman. You, on the other hand…"

"Mother…" Stella begged.

"No daughter of mine will act so common. It's my fault, really. Your father and I spoiled you three." Her mother shook her head. "Ambrose never had the taste for rebellion that you did, and Euphemia is too young to think about such things."

Stella glanced away, trying to put physical distance between them. Mentally, she knew her mother would never hit her—it wasn't ladylike—but at that moment, Ethel Craven seemed capable of murder.

"You are a woman now," her mother continued. "It is time you act like one."

Stella bit her tongue until tears welled up in her eyes. She fought the urge to reply. Anything she said would just make it all worse.

"You have a duty to this family. I expect you to fulfill it."

With that, her mother walked from the room, trailing disappointment behind her.

Stella collapsed into the chair by the window. She flinched as Jeanette approached her.

The maid must have seen. Jeanette stopped in her tracks and moved to the trunk instead. The distance helped. Stella could barely breathe. Having Jeanette so close just made everything worse since everything that happened would just be reported back to her mother later.

"Were they really so bad, miss? Her ladyship and Lord Pemberton? If you don't mind me asking?"

Stella shook her head. Her stomach turned. "The Countess seemed nice enough. We don't have a lot in common, but she seemed friendly. But Lord Pemberton, that man is a menace!"

Her maid picked up the dresses, smoothing them as she hung them once more. "Is he cruel? Some of the other maids said that some of the American brides got treated awfully by these Brits."

Stella sighed and pressed her fingers into her temples.

"He led me to believe he was someone else. I told him everything. Calvin, the letter, Mother, all of it."

He hadn't been cruel, and he could have easily told her mother what she had said. But how could she ever trust him after he omitted his identity like that? Looking back now, it was clear that he knew who she was, and he never once mentioned that she was talking about him.

"Letter, miss?"

She jerked upright. Her throat tightened. Jeanette didn't know about Cal's letter.

"I'm sorry, miss. It's not my place to ask."

Stella shook her head. She desperately needed someone to talk to about this. It would be easier if she knew she could trust Jeanette. It was a shame Stella felt that way as Jeanette had worked for the Craven family for nearly ten years and had been Stella's maid for nearly four years.

It was a risk to trust her but one she desperately needed to take. "If I show you something, you can't mention it to my mother or Blakely."

"I won't say anything to Mrs. Craven."

It was as good of a promise as she was going to get.

She stood up, reaching for her purse, feeling for the envelope inside. She handed it to Jeanette, who opened it with a curious look.

"Cal was going to take me to New York."

She heard Jeanette's sharp intake of breath before she dared to look at the maid. "Miss Stella! This is weeks from now."

"Cal's coming over here first, and then he'll accompany me back."

Her eyes went wide, and Stella wondered if Jeanette might pass out

"It's romantic," she tried to argue, though none of it had anything to do with romance. The idea of romance with Cal seemed like such a far-fetched notion. "It'll be like a story."

Jeanette handed her the envelope, a frown on her face as she moved to the door. "I hope so, miss."

"You can't tell my mother," she pleaded. Her eyes watered at the thought. Jeanette paused, nodding before she left.

Stella closed her eyes, already berating herself. How could she be so stupid? She already told a complete stranger everything. Telling Jeanette was just as bad. She could only pray that the girl would stay true to her vow and wouldn't say a word.

6

────────

WILLIAM

THE CAB STOPPED in front of their house, and William helped his mother out. Mother had insisted that he take her to the Covent Garden. The tickets had been a gift, and it would have been a shame to let such marvelous seats go to waste.

She took his arm, and he helped her up the stairs. She was hardly fragile, but he was always amazed that she could walk in an evening gown, just as he was always amazed that the starched collar of his shirt had never cut him.

The door opened up, and Mr. Farley stood inside, ready to take their coats.

"What did you think of Miss Craven?" his mother asked, breaching the subject for the first time since that afternoon.

What did he think of her? All he could remember was the anger in her eyes as he read her letter. The way she had waxed poetic about Carter or Calvert or whatever his name was. Her obvious disdain of him. How she had remained suspiciously quiet during tea. It was reasonable to say that there was no chance she wanted to marry him.

To be fair, he didn't want to marry her either. But he would gladly put aside his desires to do his duty to his family. If the

Cravens' money was the best way to save Wraughtley, then so be it.

"I think Miss Craven is very American."

His mother scoffed, the noise almost unusual for her.

William glanced away as Mr. Farley helped him out of his coat. "If you need me, I'll be in the study."

WILLIAM OPENED his briefcase from where he left it earlier, pulled the papers out, and spread them on the desk in the study. Everything needed to be read carefully before he explained them to his father. It was a shame that the Earl didn't care more about managing the estate. Father thought that money came in from the farms and the tenants. Tenants he didn't collect rent from every month if they couldn't afford it because he didn't want to waste energy tracking them down. They were insignificant compared to him, and that's why he had a son to deal with the day to day collection for the estate. It allowed his father to look the part of the kindly lord while he gambled away what money did come in, placing the burden of managing the finances on William.

The estate had taxes to pay. They couldn't afford to keep allowing tenants to not pay their rent. He clenched the handle of the case tight enough to leave impressions before he forced himself to set it back down. Being angry about their circumstances would not accomplish anything.

Running through the numbers again, there was no feasible way to keep the entire estate intact. Large portions of the land hadn't been used in years and weren't viable for farming or livestock. No income was being made from those parcels, and it would be best to get rid of them before the land depreciated completely in value.

He heard his mother walk in and sit down on the sofa

behind him, but he didn't look up from what he was doing before he started talking. "My meeting with Mr. Moore was a success. He granted us a small loan."

"That sounds like good news."

He glanced back at her. "By my calculations, it should keep us afloat for another couple months."

His stomach turned at the thought. That was only a few months to figure out how to pay back the bank. The best option would be to sell off those plots of the land. He didn't want to approach his father with that option, but now it was necessary.

"That sounds like news we can tell your father."

He bit the lip. He didn't want to tell his father. He already knew how he'd react.

"Tell me what?"

William went still and took a deep breath before he turned around. In the doorway, the Earl of Wraughtley stood like the Ghost of Christmas Future. A harsh shadow from the lamp cut across his face. Automatically, William glanced down and gathered his courage before he could speak.

He plastered a smile on his face as he looked up. "Good news, Father," he started. It felt like he was ordering his own execution. "The bank granted us another loan."

"Another?"

If words were knives, his father spoke that one sharp enough to kill. William swallowed, trying not to show any weakness. Like any predator, Edward Pemberton could smell fear. It always amazed him that his mother and father managed to get along. He couldn't imagine two more different people in all of England.

"What is this family coming to?"

His mother stood and moved quietly towards his father. She reached out and touched his arm soothingly. "Edward, darling, this is good news." His father scoffed. "Our son worked very hard to get this loan."

The Earl sighed, and William relaxed as he saw some of the anger leave the man.

"I understand that." His father stepped inside the room. His mother's hand slipped from his shoulder. "Well, let's hear it. How much?"

"Enough for about two months' expenses."

His father nodded. He stared like he was attempting to bore a hole into William. When he spoke, his voice was back to ice. "And after two months?"

"We're on our own."

William turned to the desk and grabbed the appropriate papers. He offered them to the Earl, who took them and began looking them over.

William swallowed as he prepared himself to deliver the next bit of news.

"In the meantime, we should begin selling some of these smaller plots of land. They aren't viable for farming, and no one lives on them."

His father glanced up, his displeasure at the idea clear on his face.

"I don't like it. Find some other way."

William could read the words his father didn't say: this would make the Earl appear weak. He swallowed hard as his father stood and left the room, signalling that there would be no more discussion on this matter.

His mother offered him a consolatory smile. "I'm sorry that didn't go the way you hoped, Pem. Marrying Miss Craven is simply the best solution."

For a brief second, a flash of anger shot through him. Why did she always apologize for everything his father did?

Ice ran through his blood. He should have known better

than to hope that anything would change. They were right back where they started."

SEVERAL HOURS LATER AND WILLIAM, hunched over the desk, still hadn't found another solution to the problem. In the dying light, the words on the page seemed to taunt him. His glasses slipped down his nose, and he pulled them off, dropping them on the desk. He blinked and fought the strain he felt from wearing them for so long.

"Pemmy?" a voice asked from behind him. He jumped, reaching for his glasses to slide them back on his face. His mother sat on the sofa in her dressing gown. Her hair was loose. *She must be heading to bed*, he thought.

"Mother!" He did his best to school his expression. He almost felt guilty, but there was no reason why he should. "I didn't hear you come in."

"Why are you still awake?"

"Just reading this. I'll head to bed in a few minutes."

He fought back a yawn at his words as he turned back to the papers. He didn't want to forget altogether where he had been. He had wanted to make a note, but she had made him lose the thought.

His mother sighed loudly. Her soft footsteps crunched on the carpet as she placed her hand on his chair.

"I know it is a lot to ask from you, but please give Miss Craven a chance."

What?

He set his pen down and glanced up at her. Where had the topic of Miss Craven come from? He hadn't mentioned her in hours. To be honest, he had tried to put her from his mind.

"To do what, Mother?"

She turned away from him. He twisted in his seat to watch

her. She stayed quiet, examining the shelves and doing every-thing she could not to look at him. What was she thinking?

"You should marry her." Her words came so suddenly that he couldn't follow what she was talking about. *Marry Miss Craven?*

"But she's already engaged," he muttered, but it was clear his mother didn't hear him because she continued without stopping.

"Perhaps by marrying her, you wouldn't have to worry so much." He pulled his glasses off and pinched the bridge of his nose to try to stave off the headache forming as he turned back to the desk. "Don't stay up too late." He felt her hand on his back for a second. "Good night, Pemmy."

"Of course not," he said softly without looking up. "Good night, Mother."

The hand was gone, and she closed the door as she left.

Marry Miss Craven?

Marrying her wouldn't solve anything. She would have to be incredibly rich in order for it to make a difference. An American woman, no matter how rich, wouldn't be used to running a great house. She would be used to a different way of life. She had a man she loved waiting for her. It wasn't fair to ask her to give all of that up.

Even if it was his family that would suffer.

7

———

STELLA

THE FRANCO-BRITISH EXHIBITION was more crowded than during Stella's previous visits. It was unseasonably chilly for June, or at least, that was what she heard. The rain, thankfully, held off. The word had gotten out, and people started pouring in, filling the booths so that it was impossible to get in. Their voices merged together like a roar, making one indistinguishable from the next.

Unlike her tea outfit, Stella had selected an appropriate cream-colored walking suit. She wasn't trying to make any political statements. Her mother was finally letting her out of her sight. She supposed after the debacle at tea, she couldn't stand to be around her. That suited Stella just fine.

Jeanette was dressed tastefully, better than half of the women at the showcase who wore their best rags. She wore a plain, light green dress—one of Stella's old dresses that she somehow wore better than Stella ever had.

In the canal, small rowboats filled with couples passed by. Men in suits strolled next to lace-clad women, staring adoringly at each other. Everywhere she went was a reminder of what she was supposed to be like.

Stella closed her eyes and took a deep breath as she tried to forget all of that. She wanted to enjoy the day, not be bogged down by the weight of her responsibilities. She wouldn't let William Pemberton and their mothers ruin yet another day.

"Thank you for allowing me to accompany you, miss," Jeanette said softly, drawing Stella from her thoughts.

Stella shook her head. "Not at all." She grinned at the maid. "You're better company than my mother." And her mother wouldn't let her leave the hotel without supervision, like she was afraid that Stella would disappear from England if she was left unsupervised for one moment.

It wasn't like she could escape to Southampton and stay there for a month while she waited for Cal. She had no money of her own, and the police would probably find her in days.

She was almost jealous of Jeanette. Jeanette could leave her job if she wanted. She could marry who she'd like. She could do as she pleased. She was free in a way that Stella never would be, without any restraints to hold her back.

In her mother's mind, Stella was running away from marriage, but she wasn't. She would be happy to marry the right man when it was the right time. But that wasn't now, and wasn't Lord Pemberton or anyone with 'Lord' attached to their surname.

Stella blinked and glanced away. She didn't want Jeanette to see too much on her face. She wasn't in love with Cal, not the way people talked about in stories. It was nice being around him. He was always supportive of her and everything she did. It wasn't like being around her parents.

Stella paused and stared at the Palace of Woman's Work, a grand white building, like almost every other one that was there. Its only distinguishing features were the two ornate towers and lakeside position. A boat passed under a white bridge that crossed over the small canal next to the building. She leaned on the railing to get a better view.

"I want freedom, Jeanette." She glanced back at the girl. "I want to be able to choose my husband. Why should my parents decide who I will spend the rest of my life with?"

Jeanette stepped up to the railing and looked Stella in the eyes for a change. "Even if it's the wrong person?"

"Then it'll have been my choice and mine alone. My mistakes to make. Isn't that what we're fighting for?"

"Miss, are you still involved with those suffragists?" The maid's tone was heavy with disapproval, and Stella looked away. "Please be careful, Miss Stella. I've read that many women have been imprisoned for just attending the rallies."

"That's hardly true," she muttered as she straightened her jacket. That was a lie, and they both knew it. She didn't want anyone worrying more about her. "Besides, even if I wanted to be involved with such a cause, I wouldn't be allowed since it goes against the wishes of my dear mother, who would be terribly embarrassed if I were arrested at such an event."

With that, Stella turned and began walking again. Her mother would lock her in her room for the rest of her life if she thought there was the slightest possibility that Stella attended any such meetings. Her mother thought Stella only did any of this just to be a nuisance. Why should Stella believe in a cause greater than herself?

Behind her, Jeanette's boots clicked briskly on the stone pavement as Stella headed towards the bridge. Stella straightened and held herself proudly as she walked along the waterway and kept moving. Jeanette stayed a few paces back, as though she might catch Stella's desire for independence if she got too close.

Well, Stella would have to do something about that.

She made a sharp turn towards the Palace of Woman's Work. The last time she was there, she wanted to see it, but her mother had forbidden it, too afraid Stella might get more ideas. She shook her head. That was ridiculous.

Stella stepped inside the building and paused. Jeanette followed and apologized to the people she bumped into.

Paintings of women lined the walls. They farmed the land, spun wool, and wove, among the other jobs that women worked at for centuries.

Woman's work. Stella shook her head.

She doubted many knew that knitting and weaving had guilds during the Middle Ages. Like most guilds in that time, women weren't generally admitted. Guilds were for highly skilled tradesmen, and therefore, most only accepted men.

The whole exhibit made her sick. It wasn't a novelty to be gawked at. Jeanette worked. Thousands of other women worked. And yet, none of them were considered equal to their male counterparts. It wasn't fair.

Jeanette stared at her, but Stella ignored her as she looked around the room. "I want my daughters to have a place in this world, as more than a daughter or a wife or a mother."

"That sounds very noble."

Stella smiled. It did sound noble.

"I want to be brave like my aunt." She glanced at her maid. "Did you know she used to race cars? She was widowed young and never remarried. She toured Europe and answered to no one."

Her aunt died a few years before, but she was everything Stella wanted to be. Jeanette squeezed her arm, and Stella reached up to pat her hand.

"Miss Craven!" a voice called from behind. Stella flinched as she recognized its owner. "What a surprise!"

Jeanette's fingers fell away as Stella turned to see Lord Pemberton approach them. She straightened. This was the last place she expected to see him, and she didn't really feel like dealing with him.

"Lord Pemberton, so nice to see you again."

His eyes went over her shoulder for a moment, towards

Jeanette, before the maid spoke, "My lord, Miss Craven, if you will please excuse me."

With that, the girl's footsteps hurried away from them.

"I didn't expect to see you again so soon."

"Yes, well... I apologize. I very much enjoyed our meeting."

Stella rolled her eyes. She very much doubted that. "You enjoyed watching me make a fool out of myself, you mean?"

"Not at all." *Was he saying that just to be contrary?* "It would be ridiculous to think that you haven't found a man who already adores you."

She glanced away. Adored was a strong word. It was hard to imagine Cal adoring anything but the law. He could wax poetic for days about the American justice system. She never heard him talk about her like that.

But Lord Pemberton seemed oblivious to her reactions, carrying on as if he was the only one that mattered. "Have you been here already?"

"Twice now."

"Then you wouldn't mind showing me around? I doubt I'll find another guide as lovely as you."

His tone was flirtatious, and Stella couldn't help but glare at him. Nearly every English aristocrat she had met on this trip had the same entitled, arrogant attitude. Lord Pemberton radiated it, and yet, her mother and Jeanette both seemed charmed by it.

He offered her his arm. She hoped that her smile didn't look too much like a grimace.

"It would be my pleasure," she told him as she took the viscount's arm, though she could think of any number of things that would be more pleasurable.

They strolled around the room and paused briefly at each painting and display before moving on.

"You don't like me very much," he said, catching her by surprise. "Do you?"

Stella swallowed. "I'm sure you're a perfectly lovely person."

She was taken aback when Lord Pemberton laughed, loudly and with his whole body, the vibrations traveling through his arm and into her hand. She glanced up at him and was surprised by the mirth in his eyes. His laugh was actually pleasant to listen to, and the answering grin that spread across her face had no need to be faked.

"How do you know? I could be a perfectly awful one?"

She stayed silent. Anything she said would probably ruin the lighter mood between them, and for some reason, that was the last thing she wanted.

"Have you eaten?" he asked abruptly.

"Not yet."

He glanced at his watch and then tucked it back into his pocket. "Would you care to join me for lunch?"

"It would be my pleasure." This time when she spoke the words, she actually meant them.

"I'VE NEVER HAD lunch alone with a man before," Stella said, glancing around the restaurant a bit anxiously, "At least, not with a man that I wasn't related to."

Her mother would go mad if she knew.

Lord Pemberton stared at the place setting in front of him and refused to look up. She couldn't blame him. The whole situation was beyond awkward.

"I used to go to lunch with my sister at the tearoom in Wraughtley."

"Used to?" she asked. "What changed?"

"She decided that she was too mature. She was presented this year."

Stella nodded. The British were so strange with these

things. If you were a lady, you had to be presented at court before you could go to the parties and balls that were any good. At least, that had been Stella's understanding of it. Her mother had convinced her Aunt Vivien, who was the dowager Countess of Astermore, to be Stella's escort when she was presented to the king and queen of England.

"She's having her ball next weekend," he said with a roll of his eyes. "I'm sure my mother already sent you an invite."

"I'm sure she did. My mother handles all of that. I just show up where she tells me when she tells me."

Lord Pemberton chuckled at that. "Then does she know that you're here?"

That dragged a laugh out of her. When he wasn't surrounded by those meddling women, he wasn't so bad.

"No, and I doubt she would approve. An unchaperoned lunch." She gasped. "How unthinkable!"

He smiled. He had a nice smile when he wasn't smirking. She had been so determined to hate him for the sake of hating him that she never gave him a chance to be nice to her.

Not that he made the best first impression either by reading her mail or criticizing her for hiding.

"Your tea, my lord, miss." A waiter set a steaming pot on the table. Lord Pemberton poured some into his cup before spooning half of the pot of sugar and pouring a disgusting amount of milk into the cup.

Stella poured some for herself and drank. She was unsuccessful at keeping the grimace off of her face.

"Not a fan of tea?" The smug look on his face had returned.

"Not particularly." She eyed the nearly white liquid in his cup. "I see you aren't either."

"If I'm being honest," he leaned in like he was telling her a big secret, "I prefer coffee."

"With as much sugar and milk as you can fit in the cup, I'm sure."

His eyes narrowed, and he waved one of the waiters over.

"I need a fresh cup," he said, glaring indignantly across the table at Stella. "My hand slipped."

"Right away, my lord." The waiter bowed slightly before spiriting away the cup and saucer.

"What exactly are you hoping to prove?" She leaned back slightly in the chair. Every inch of physical distance between them helped to clear her head like a splash of cold water to her face. She couldn't think straight around him. He flustered her.

"I'm not sure yet." An empty cup appeared before him, along with a stream of apologies. Lord Pemberton ignored the waiter in favor of pouring the tea into his cup, taking a sip with nothing in it. He fought well to keep the grimace off of his face, but the shudder that accompanied the pained expression gave him away. "We could be friends, you know?"

Stella fought back a snort. "I very much doubt that my mother would approve or appreciate me just being friends with you."

His expression darkened slightly. The look in his eyes scared her. "No, I imagine not. She, like my mother, wants us to marry." Stella swallowed and refused to move her eyes from her cup. "Am I correct?"

"Yes."

He was watching her. She could feel his predatory gaze bearing down on her. She risked a glance up at him through her lashes. When she was younger, her family had a cat that used to get loose. He would stalk into the alleyways and chase mice with the exact same look on his face.

But he was not a cat, and she was not a mouse.

She gathered her courage and raised her head completely.

"Am I mistaken in saying you don't wish to marry me?" Lord Pemberton asked.

She bit her lip, hating how easily her emotions showed on her face.

"I'm sure you'll make a wonderful husband," she started with no real idea where she was going.

But he knew. "Just not for you."

She didn't dare speak. Whatever she said would only make everything worse.

"Because of your fiancé or because of you?"

She hesitated for a moment. "Both."

He nodded slowly, like a man who had very little hope that she'd say anything different.

"Please don't misunderstand," she continued as her courage grew. "I think we'd both be perfectly miserable together."

Anyone buried under that many expectations would have to be.

"I understand." She was taken aback by how light he sounded, as if they were discussing the weather. "I don't want to marry you either. I'd like to not marry anyone at all."

It struck her funny how much his words stung. Why should she care what he thought?

I don't.

But she did. Since they met, she had been unable to remove him from her mind.

His words hurt. Her chest felt like it wasn't expanding enough to get air, but she refused to let him see how his words affected her. She was not some swooning maiden who needed to toss herself at his feet.

He finished his food and quickly paid for both of their meals before he stood.

"I enjoyed our chat. I'm sure we'll see each other again soon, Miss Craven."

"I'm sure."

Other patrons' eyes bore holes into her skin as he walked

away. She gathered her things. She needed to be anywhere but there.

Sweeping from the cafe, she set out to find Jeanette and found her sitting on a bench outside.

"The nerve of that man!" she declared.

"Miss?"

"He... he told me he doesn't want to marry me."

Why the words stung the way they did, she wasn't sure.

"But, miss, you didn't want to marry him either."

Stella bit her lip and turned her head so that she didn't have to meet the other girl's eyes. Jeanette had a way of making her feel like she was a child.

"It's just—" She cut herself off. She hated the way her eyes teared up out of frustration. She sounded ridiculous. She felt ridiculous and was proving her mother right. She was irresponsible. "It's not exactly something anyone wants to hear."

She turned on her heel at that, not caring if Jeanette followed her or not.

AWAY FROM THE CROWDS, it was easier to breathe. It felt less like everyone's eyes were trained on her, waiting for her to react to the obvious humiliation she had suffered.

Why was she so upset about a man she didn't want anything to do with in the first place?

It was irrational, to be honest. She felt like she was drowning, and everyone was standing to watch.

The bridge led away from the Palace of Woman's Work, away from the cafe, towards an area where she was able to sit down and take a few deep breaths.

As always, Jeanette hovered behind her. Her presence was comforting despite the fact Stella knew her mother would hear about her afternoon breakdown.

"I hate England." The maid stayed silent. "I can't wait to leave. I don't think I ever want to return here."

Why didn't Cal book an earlier date? She would have been fine to travel alone.

"But what about Mrs. Craven?"

Stella shook her head. "Nothing I do will make her happy. It's a good thing that she has another daughter who lives to please." She shuddered.

Jeanette frowned and sat down beside her on the bench. The two of them stayed silent and watched the people stroll by, lost in their own worlds.

Stella swallowed hard. She didn't need Lord Pemberton. It would be easy to walk away from him and never see him again.

So why couldn't she?

For some reason, the other option, running to Cal, was nowhere near as satisfying of an ending. If the two of them went away together, she would probably never hear from her family again. She had always been rash, but that seemed a bit extreme to her. If she had her way, she'd marry no one at all.

8

———

WILLIAM

AS HE TURNED his back and walked away, William fought the urge to turn around. The way Miss Craven's expression crumpled almost did him in. He wanted to tell her that he didn't mean it, but he wouldn't beg. Apologize for the harsh way he had presented his words, but he would not be reduced to a sniveling shell of a man. He had too much pride for that.

He watched as Miss Craven approached her companion from earlier. Her face was like thunderclouds, darkened from the humiliating blow he had delivered her. The companion stood as Stella stormed away, and it was only then that he realized what he had done. His damned, foolish pride had gotten him nowhere.

Stella Craven did not need him. He had no doubts that she had received better offers from men of higher ranks and less desperate situations.

But if Wraughtley Hall was to survive in the coming years, he needed her.

William swallowed, his throat tightening.

"Sir?" a man's voice asked softly. He paused before William. "Are you all right?"

"Not at all." He looked up. "I think I just ruined everything."

"Sir?"

William shook his head. "Never mind. There's nothing you can do. There's nothing anyone can do."

The man gave him an odd look before he continued on his way.

Damn her, he thought, barely stopping himself from pulling at his hair. And damn himself for mucking up a perfectly civil afternoon with talk of marriage.

He hated Cal, whoever he was. Cal must be incredible to convince Stella to marry him.

Stella Craven was not the weak-minded society girl who dreamed of her wedding and giggled when men approached her. She would not be swayed by the idea of moving to a country estate any more than she would the idea of bearing a title. If he wanted to win her over, he'd have to figure out something she'd actually want.

But it would take time, which he definitely didn't have.

THE ROYAL ASCOT, in William's opinion, was perhaps the most important event of the Season. He had never been much of a gambler—though his father was—but every year, the young lord placed the bare minimum on a horse. Something about having a horse to root for made the whole experience more exciting.

That day, he clung to the ticket for a horse called Red Diamond being jockeyed by Danny Maher, an American who had won the race two years before. From his vantage point at the fence, he could see Miss Craven and her mother. Miss Craven wore a white gown, tight in places to the point it was almost indecent, and a large purple hat with great plumes attached to the brim. She was magnificent, and William was hit with another pang of longing. It was no use pining for a woman who was in love with another man, but it was like his losing ticket. He just couldn't help himself.

"Pem!"

William jerked his head around until he found the source of the voice. It didn't take long, not with the crowd telling the man to be quiet as he elbowed his way through. Albert Rutledge was a school friend and was one of the few who knew him as William before his grandfather died and his father became the Earl of Wraughtley. Of all of their classmates, Bertie was perhaps the only one who hadn't ascended in status through his family name or titles. Instead, he forged his path to fortune by owning a string of successful magazines. William envied him.

"Sorry," Bertie apologized as he pushed towards the front. "Sorry. Your parents said you were this way."

He stopped by William's side. Beyond him, William caught a glimpse of Stella's face as she turned towards the starting line.

"Who's she?"

William jerked and tore his gaze away. "Who?"

"The lady you were staring at."

William glanced towards the gates where the horses were lining up.

"You always pick such odd ones," Bertie said as he ripped the ticket from William's hand. "Here. Take mine."

"I can't do that."

"I insist. Because I'm going to cheer on Red Diamond now." He shook his head. He saw what everyone saw in Bertie. He was confident, so sure of everything.

"The White Knight," William read aloud. "Didn't he win last year?"

Bertie grinned.

William turned back as the horses left the gates. Red Diamond was behind, pulling forward, faster, faster. The crowd leaned forward. All wanted to see their pick win.

The White Knight pulled ahead and crossed the finish line seconds before any of the others. William stared at the ticket, then at Bertie.

"You won."

His friend shook his head. "No. That's my gift to you. A birthday gift if you'd like."

William swallowed, almost uncomfortable with the idea of taking money from his friend. But his pride had gotten him in enough trouble for one week. Besides, Bertie would take offense to him rejecting a birthday gift.

Bertie grinned. "You can use it to take the lady you keep staring at out to dinner or the theater."

William shook his head. "I haven't been staring at anyone."

"Then you won't mind if I go talk to the lovely creature in the purple hat."

Panic shot through him as Bertie turned to leave. He gripped the other man's arm tightly, though he did his best not to cause a scene.

"No," he hissed. His fingers dug into his friend's sleeve. A smirk spread across Bertie's face, and William loosened his grip.

"So you do care." William pressed his lips together. Bertie sighed. "Who is she?"

"Her name is Stella Craven. She's American, and she hates me."

Bertie's gaze danced back towards Stella. William fought the urge to look again. She hadn't peeked in his direction once in the entire time he had been there. It felt deliberate on her part, like she was actively avoiding him, and it shocked him how much it annoyed him.

"What did you do?"

He glared at his friend. "Nothing. I didn't even have to meet her for my presence to offend her."

Bertie seemed like he wanted to say something, but he refrained.

"Our mothers wished for us to marry." William glanced at the track. "I don't know what they were thinking."

"She doesn't want to marry you? Why?" If they had been talking about any other woman, William might have smiled at the outrage that colored his friend's tone. "What lady would pass up the chance at a young, titled noble? There's only so many of you around."

"She told me we'd be miserable together."

That was what really hurt. She seemed so certain that they were destined to fail that she wasn't willing to give him a chance. Not that he should have cared. There was just something about her that made him act irrationally. The whole marriage affair should have been treated like the business transaction that it was.

He glanced down at his hands. His knuckles were white, clenched to the railing, and he forced them open.

"You don't think so?" Bertie asked softly.

William looked at Stella, who had finally turned her head in his direction. Their eyes met for a split second, and he could see the way she reacted to being caught. She jerked her head, and her hat's massive brim separated them once more.

"It doesn't really matter what I think."

Stella wasn't like all the ladies he was used to dealing with. She wouldn't be so easily swayed. But she was still in England, so perhaps he had a chance to convince her to stay.

9

———

STELLA

THE FLOOR WAS SPOTTED with a sea of colorful spinning silk-clad women. Stella clutched her hands tighter. As they waited in line, her nerves ate at her. Lord and Lady Wraughtley stood beside a girl Stella assumed was the Lady Margaret Pemberton. She was an unassuming girl like the ones Stella passed dozens of times on the street. She wore an equally unspectacular gown that was pretty in a plain sort of way. If this was her ball, wouldn't she want to make a statement?

Stella's mother stood proudly before her. She inched anxiously forward to greet the family. Stella took some relief in the fact that Lord Pemberton wasn't with the rest of his family.

"It's lovely to see you again, Countess." Her mother curtsied to the other woman.

"And you, Mrs. Craven, and Miss Craven. Have you met my husband, the Earl of Wraughtley?" She motioned to the man beside her, and they traded how do you dos. "And my daughter, Lady Margaret."

Stella moved through the motions, saying what she hoped were the right things in the right places. She didn't feel like herself. She felt like she was a child again and was supposed to be a piece of art to show off. Only this was worse. She was hiding from Lord Pemberton because she felt foolish. Why should he want to marry her when she acted like this?

"Miss Craven?" Stella flinched as she heard the voice. The Honorable Archibald Bramley, son of Baron Something or Another, had spotted her. He stalked towards her the same way a predator did their prey. She swallowed and tried to prepare herself mentally for the riveting presence of a man who thought he was God's gift to American heiresses. According to the gossip she'd heard, she was his third victim this year.

"Mr. Bramley." She prayed the man would get the hint to leave her alone. He did not.

"You look stunning tonight. We should dance."

With no further ado, she found herself dragged onto the dance floor. Fortunately for her, it was one of the livelier sets, which severely limited Bromley's ability to talk. Still, she admired his attempts.

"You look to be in fine health this evening."

"Thank you."

"I too am in fine health," Mr. Bromley declared.

She pressed her lips together in an attempt to stifle the laugh that threatened to break forth.

"You do seem quite well."

He puffed at that, reminding Stella of the peacocks at her cousins' country home, all fluffing their magnificent tails to try and attract the hens. She suspected she and Mr. Bromley were not of the same species. Perhaps that was why he had no effect on her other than disdain.

"I keep in shape by playing cricket and rowing. Do you plan on seeing the Olympic rowing events in a few weeks?"

"I'm not sure."

"You should go. I'm especially looking forward to the coxless pairs."

"I'm afraid I have no idea what that means," she told him in hopes that it would deter him.

He grinned, and Stella fought the urge to shudder.

"It refers to the design of the boat." She nodded, though she didn't actually understand or care, and he continued on. "One of the competitors, Philip Verdon, went to Westminster school with me. I am very much looking forward to seeing him compete."

"I'm sure."

The music changed, but Mr. Bromley paid no attention.

"Of course, it is a shame that the Olympic Committee does not classify cricket as one of their sports."

She made a sympathetic noise. Cricket was a foreign concept to her. She thought it was something like baseball, but the first man she said that to had gotten rather angry at the idea when she suggested that.

Stella, Cal, and their friend Rebecca Russell used to go to baseball games together. They went to every game in the 1906 World Series, and Stella was incredibly disappointed when the Chicago Cubs lost to the Chicago White Sox. Their win made no sense to her, but Cal had been excited. The White Sox were his team, while she and Rebecca both rooted for the Cubs.

Last year, Cal was at school and was unable to come home for the World Series, so Ambrose went with her and Rebecca. They weren't able to go to all of the games—two of them were played in Detroit, and there was no way that Stella's mother would allow her to go so far to watch a sport—but since the Cubs won, she had been excited.

She was disappointed she wouldn't get to go to any games this year. She hoped that the Olympics would make up for it.

Mr. Bromley continued his rant without ever noticing Stella was no longer listening. "It is a gentleman's sport, though. I'm sure they were trying to keep things simple. They've even let the Irish compete!"

As if that explained anything. She was sure her Irish grandmother would find fault with Bromley's declaration.

"Excuse me."

"Lord Pemberton!" Bramley exclaimed.

"Do you mind if I cut in?" Lord Pemberton asked. "Miss Craven promised me this dance."

Stella wondered if the relief showed on her face. Mr. Bramley colored and released her. He stammered an apology to the young lord before he moved onto his next victim of the evening.

"Thank you for your assistance, Lord Pemberton. Now if you don't mind..." She trailed off as she attempted to make her escape, but he foiled her plans by blocking her path.

"I do believe you owe me a dance."

She swallowed and glared up at him. It would be rude to leave after he'd saved her from Bramley the Boor, especially since it'd give away his lie. She sighed and nodded. "One dance."

She didn't think she could do too much damage in that time.

He held his hand out to her, and together, they moved among the other couples. One hand rested lightly on her back, and the other held her gloved hand loosely as he led her in a gentle waltz. His shoulder felt solid beneath her fingers.

"Not that I'm not grateful for your help, because I am, but why did you come over when you did? How did you know?"

She winced at the way she stumbled over her words.

"You looked like you'd rather be anywhere else." His words lacked the cruel bite that another person might have had.

They spun, and her stomach flipped a little as he pulled her a bit closer than what was technically proper. She wondered if he could hear her heart racing over the music. Dancing with Cal had never felt quite like this.

No, she told herself, *don't get drawn in again.*

She never wanted to feel as humiliated as she had the other day. Allowing Lord Pemberton to get too close would lead to nothing but pain.

Still, as the song ended, she couldn't bring herself to step away from him.

"Would you like to see something interesting?" he asked as they left the dance floor.

Against her better judgment, Stella nodded, and he took her hand as he pulled her from the ballroom.

"Where—?" She cut off as he raised a finger to his lips and pushed open a door that led to narrow stairs. It was surprisingly devoid of servants.

"Where are we going?" she asked as they reached the attic and still continued on.

"You'll see."

With that, he pulled open a door into darkness and stepped through.

Her breath hitched, but Lord Pemberton stood there, hand outstretched.

"Trust me."

God help her, she did.

The rooftop air held a chill that the ballroom lacked, and she had to grab her skirts to avoid tripping on the chimneys, but she could see why he had brought her up there. The view was incredible, the kind of thing you could only picture while reading Dickens.

They weren't on the tallest building, but it wasn't the shortest either, and Stella could see for miles. She doubted anyone came up there often, so few would ever get to appreciate it.

The sun had not fully set, not with the days getting longer again, and the sky was streaked with pinks and indigos. Windows were lit up in houses, each their own miniature in the fast fading dusk. The streetlights formed flickering jewels that laced down the road and disappeared.

When she managed to tear her eyes away, Lord Pemberton was staring at her.

"I hoped you might like this."

"I do," she whispered, her fingers curling around his. "I really do."

IT WAS strange to see so many women in one place who were not attempting to outshine each other's fashions. Instead, they were all joined for a common cause. The right to vote.

It almost made Stella feel faint. Would a woman with her own rights separate from her husband or father ever be forced into her situation again?

Women dressed in whites and greens and purples conjugated around the park. Some held banners proclaiming "Votes for Women" as they cried the same.

Others handed out flyers to passersby. Stella could even see one woman standing with her head above the crowd shouting so that people could hear her. Regrettably, it was far too noisy, and Stella was too far away to hear a word the woman said.

The atmosphere was electric and alive.

"Miss Craven?" Jeanette's voice begged from behind Stella as they weaved further into the crowds. "I'm not so sure being here is a good idea."

"Don't worry."

"But your mother—"

Stella shook her head and stopped short, turning on the maid. "My mother is not to know about this. Do you understand?"

Jeanette nodded frantically. Was she afraid of Stella? Or

perhaps she was afraid for her. "Of course, miss. I would never."

Satisfied, Stella turned and continued on.

"Give women the vote!" a woman screamed from where she had tied herself to the fence railing. "Votes for women!"

The fingers on her arm made her jump. She found Jeanette pale and her eyes wide enough that Stella was surprised they hadn't fallen from the girl's skull.

"Please, Miss Stella, may we go?"

Behind them, a woman screamed. Stella jerked, turning in time to see a woman hit a policeman hard enough to knock him to the ground.

"Let's go," she ordered and pushed her maid towards the park entrance. "Hurry!"

They moved quickly through the crowds, and Stella forced down her disappointment. Perhaps her mother was right. Perhaps she was a bit too naïve about these things.

"I'm sorry," she apologized to Jeanette once they were safely away from the crowds. "I had no idea it would be like that."

Jeanette offered her a shaky smile, but it hardly made Stella feel better.

THE TEAROOM DOWNSTAIRS at the hotel was surprisingly crowded for a Monday. Yet another reason England was so foreign. At home, when Monday came, her father went to work. The men of the British upper class hardly seemed to work. Most of their jobs seemed to be socializing.

The maître d' led her inside, through the maze of tables towards one that was empty when she saw him. *Lord Pemberton.* The man who made her insides twist like a schoolgirl's. He sat studying his cup like it held all of life's answers. She wondered if he'd had any luck.

Stella paused as they passed. "Do you mind if I join you?"

After the other night, she didn't think he would. He might even welcome the company.

Lord Pemberton glanced up and motioned to the chair across from him. "Please."

The maître d' bowed his head and pulled out the chair for her. As she sat, he took his leave.

"How are you?" Lord Pemberton asked.

"I'm well."

He eyed her. "You seem a bit shaken." She shook her head. "What's wrong? You can tell me."

"But we're not friends," she protested and winced. There she was, sticking her foot into her mouth.

Lord Pemberton didn't seem offended by her words. He took them in stride, offering her that sometimes-charming smile of his.

"Ah, but we're better than friends. Who better to tell your problems to than a stranger?"

She stared at him. She supposed after two failed encounters and one lovely conversation, they were only strangers. Perhaps this was his attempt at making peace.

The waiter brought a teacup for her and a fresh plate of scones. She waited for him to leave before she spoke. "I'm just disappointed, I suppose."

Across the table, Lord Pemberton's brow furrowed. "You suppose."

His voice held no inflection whatsoever. She fought against the knot forming in her stomach and soldiered on.

"I am. I went to Hyde Park, to the rally," she tacked on, in case he hadn't followed the news. "What a mess that was."

"I read about it in the morning paper. They were throwing stones on Downing Street."

She cringed. It was fanatics like that who gave people like her a bad name. They thought violence would win freedom. It sickened her.

"I suppose I shouldn't be surprised that you are a suffragette."

Stella reached for the tea and poured herself a little.

"I thought that things would be different here. I had such romantic notions of it." She laughed a little bitterly. She thought England would be fantastic, the stuff of stories. "It's nothing like I'd imagined. Everyone here is so..." She trailed off.

He blinked. "Do you really feel so strongly about it?"

"No, not exactly." She sighed, feeling the fight go out of her. "Not the politics of it. Er—" She bit her lip. That wasn't entirely true. She didn't totally mind the politics. It was frustrating that she couldn't do anything about it. "It's a little hard to explain."

Lord Pemberton nodded slowly. "You want freedom, but without the fight for it."

She shook her head. "I want freedom, but without the violence of a revolution," she corrected. "I know that sounds silly. Childish."

She went to move her lip between her teeth again but forced herself to stop. It was a bad childhood habit, and she figured it didn't help her case.

"A bit idealistic, perhaps," Lord Pemberton countered, but he was staring at her with a strange expression she couldn't quite identify. Awe, definitely, but there was something else too. Something about it compelled her to keep talking.

"What I would really love is to have been able to go to college. To be able to do something more with my life."

Stella took a sip of tea from her cup. The liquid burnt her tongue, but she refused to flinch. She reached for a scone. His fingers collided with hers. It felt almost electric. Sparks raced up into her arm. Her eyes went wide, and she jerked her hand back.

"Sorry," he muttered.

For the rest of tea, Lord Pemberton wouldn't meet her eyes.

10

STELLA

A WEEK LATER, after another night of endless balls and dancing and curtsying, Stella found herself back downstairs in Claridge's tearoom. The food was tasty, and her mother found it acceptable for her to be alone there.

It was relatively quiet that morning, though it was hardly surprising. Most had danced the night away. Even her mother was still upstairs resting her eyes. A few small groups sat together, but several young ladies sat alone, sipping their tea and enjoying their relative independence.

Stella brought the newspaper for company and had just reached the section where they had printed the scores for the Wimbledon Women's Tennis. Charlotte Cooper Sterry won. Stella had started following Mrs. Cooper Sterry's career when she became the first female tennis champion at the 1900 Paris Olympics. This year's Olympics were being held in London. Stella hoped to attend some of the events before her departure.

"Miss Craven."

"Lord Pemberton!" she exclaimed as she looked up from her paper and saw the man looming over her. "What a surprise."

He laughed a bit awkwardly. "Not really. I was just here the other day."

She motioned to the empty chair across from her. "Would you care to join me?"

"With pleasure." He sat down. "You looked magnificent at the ball last night."

Stella felt the heat rising in her cheeks. She had worn a shimmering sapphire Delphos gown.

"I didn't think you noticed." She hoped she didn't sound too jealous. He spent most of the night with the Stanhope girl, Lyonesse or something to that effect. It had been the girl's ball. Of course all of the men would want to dance with her.

"Lyona is a lovely girl. She went to school with Margaret."

It took her a second to remember who Margaret was. Lady Margaret. His sister.

"Were you jealous?" he teased as he caught her look.

She laughed, but it sounded hollow to her ears.

"So, how is your morning going?"

"Well, I think. This is the first time I've been alone in days." He raised his brows at that. She folded the paper and leaned closer. "Mother's gotten it into her head that I'm going to run off."

"I wonder where she could have gotten such an idea. Could it be that she saw a certain letter in your possession?"

His words were spoken jokingly, but Stella felt a jolt of panic rush through her gut. Could her mother have seen the letter?

Perhaps Jeanette had snitched. She swallowed hard. "I rather hope not."

She tried to compose herself, and she suspected she was successful since he didn't comment. Instead, he smiled a little crookedly as he leaned in conspiratorially and asked, "Would you like to do something crazy?"

She grinned.

THE RIDE OVER WAS STRANGE. She'd never been in a carriage alone with a man.

Unlike the other times she had been at the Exhibition, it was relatively empty. Beside her, Lord Pemberton wore a hat. It wasn't like it was the first time she'd seen him wear one, but this particular hat looked rather attractive on him. It framed his face just right. Stella found herself glancing away, feeling a little shocked that she'd think of him that way.

He had offered her a hand when she climbed from the carriage and then his arm as they walked into the Exhibition. And while she had taken the help leaving the cab, it was better that they kept their distance. It felt a little cold and more than a bit lonely, but she would not be the one to say anything.

After all, he had rejected her, not the other way around.

"If anyone asks—" she started to say as she eyed the others at the Exhibition but trailed off when she couldn't quite figure out what to say.

"We could just say we're married," he teased with a little smirk quirking up the corner of his lips. She stiffened and glared at him, but it lacked the heat that it would have had last week. He pressed his lips together to stifle his laughter. "It's a perfectly reasonable explanation." He caught her eye. "Besides, no one's going to ask."

She scoffed and glanced around. It felt like everyone was watching her, no, watching them. She kept expecting to turn her head and see her mother hovering over her shoulder.

"If my mother found out where I am..."

Her mother would be ecstatic that she was getting along with Lord Pemberton. But at the same time, her mother would be furious that it had taken her so long to get to that point. The fact that Mrs. Craven had no idea where her daughter was at that moment and with whom would have driven her mother mad.

"Mine too, no doubt."

"Are we horrible children?"

"To go against conventions like this?" he asked dryly. "Yes, we are. Awful."

She lasted for only a few seconds before she burst into laughter. Lord Pemberton didn't last much longer, and Stella had to steady herself against him. It was strange how natural it felt to hold onto him.

But then he glanced at her, and his smirk faded into something softer. It felt like she was the center of his world. When he spoke again, it wasn't in the boisterous tone from before. "There's no one I'd rather be more awful with than you."

With that, he moved closer, his head tilting ever so slightly. She leaned in like two magnets drawing closer, as they—

A shriek sent them both jerking backwards as she ripped her hand from his arm. What was she doing? Lord Pemberton only tolerated her presence. They weren't... she wasn't...

She shook her head, trying to clear it. A woman tripped on the sidewalk and appeared to be the source of the scream. A number of gallant men had rushed to her rescue. From the angle of the woman's leg, her fall looked like a deliberate cry for attention. Stella didn't want to be like that woman.

"Perhaps I'm not as much of a rebel as I thought," she muttered under her breath. She barely heard Lord Pemberton's reply.

"Perhaps I'm more of one."

This time though, when he offered her his arm, she took it.

THE BLACK HORSE-DRAWN carriage pulled up to the hotel, another reminder of how different their worlds were.

Another reason a relationship with him was a bad idea. As much as Stella enjoyed London and seeing its many sites, she had yet to see any reason to stay. She would be thousands of miles away from everyone she knew, effectively trapped in a strange place alone with a man she couldn't even call by his first name.

Lord Pemberton climbed down as the cab stopped and offered her his hand. On solid ground again, they walked side by side to the doorway, like two strangers who couldn't even meet each other's eyes. The doorman opened the door for her, and Stella took it as her cue to leave before she said or did anything she would regret. She barely set a foot inside the gilded entrance when she heard Lord Pemberton's voice behind her.

"I was wondering if you might accompany me to dinner tonight."

She smiled, even as her gut twisted. He hadn't said anything to make her think that the almost-kiss was anything more than a spur-of-the-moment accident. Still, as she turned, she saw him glancing nervously at his hands. It reminded her of a child who had spoken when they didn't mean to. It was almost endearing.

"That would be lovely."

He grinned, and she steeled herself against it.

"I will meet you in the lobby." There it was, back to stiff and formal like nothing had happened. But then, he took her hand and brought it quickly to his lips. "Until tonight then."

With that, he turned and climbed back into the cab. She stood in the doorway like a fool until the cab disappeared from sight.

Why did Lord Pemberton ask her to dinner? What did he hope to accomplish?

Stella shook her head. She knew what he hoped to accomplish. A quid pro quo. He got the money needed to save his estate, he got someone to stop the countless stream of penniless ladies who wanted to marry him, and she got... she got...

Nothing. She would be stuck in a loveless marriage, doomed to be a British peer, forbidden by her would-be husband to be an activist for a cause she believed in. Her mother would be thrilled. It was everything her mother wanted for her. It would give them status with the fashionable crowd in Chicago and New York and would someday give Stella a title that her mother could boast about. A countess.

But Lord Pemberton didn't want her. He might act like he did, but she knew his survival depended on her, despite him saying otherwise. He didn't love her. But he did need her. She wanted a sign that she should walk away.

"Miss Craven!" the clerk from behind the front desk called as she passed. She paused and walked over to him. "There's a letter for you. Marked as 'Urgent.'"

Her heart flipped. It was her sign. He held the letter out to her. She asked nearly every time she passed if she had mail, and today, it finally paid off.

"Thank you." She smiled at the clerk.

Her name was written with care on the front of the envelope, but it wasn't Cal's sweeping scrawl. The postmark was from America, but the writing was much more feminine.

She turned it over. Her sister's name was on the back.

Stella took a breath and moved back over to the clerk.

"Do you have a letter opener that I can use?"

"Yes, ma'am." He passed a plain, metal opener, and she slid it through the opening. Effie hadn't written to Stella the entire time that they had been in London. Whatever it was, Effie couldn't have wanted their mother to see it. If it had been all right for their mother to see, Effie would have sent it in the same envelope with Father's letters.

Her hands shook. Anything Effie didn't want their mother to see could hardly be good news.

She unfolded it carefully.

My dearest sister Stella,

I hope you are enjoying London. I wish I could be there. I can't wait until I am able to go. Father says that when I'm old enough, I can be presented at court just like you were. Have you been to many balls since you last wrote? What have your gowns looked like?

Her stomach turned. Anytime Effie gave bad news, she always padded it with pleasantries. When she gave bad news, she wrote exactly like she spoke, overwhelming the recipient with information until you forgot why Effie was there. It would be effective if not for the fact that Stella knew that something worse lay ahead.

You'll never believe who I saw today on the way out of the theater. Calvin Wright!

Stella clutched the letter tighter. The edges crumpled in her hands as she caught the next line.

He was with the most handsome woman I've ever seen, and they were kissing. On the street, no less. I went up to him, and he introduced her as Miss Laverne Castle of Cambridge, Massachusetts. She just arrived in Chicago yesterday. Miss Castle said they're engaged. You should have seen her ring. It could sink a ship!

Engaged.

He was supposed to be engaged to her, not Miss Castle of Cambridge. They were supposed to get married. They…

The bitter, acidic taste of bile sat in the back of her throat, and she held a hand over her mouth. She wouldn't cry. She wouldn't give him the satisfaction, not in public.

They met when he was at Harvard. I can't believe it. Our Mr. Wright is finally going to settle down.

I miss you.

Your loving sister,

Effie

Effie's words mocked her from their spot on the page. He was not her anything.

Stella crushed the letter until all that remained of it was a ball of paper that she wedged into her purse. She didn't want to look at the vile thing.

A hot, wet tear trailed down her cheek, and she brushed at it frantically. She couldn't let her mother know she had been crying. Stella wouldn't give her the pleasure of knowing that she was right.

BY THE TIME she got into her room, Stella had swallowed the sharp sting of betrayal and convinced herself that she couldn't possibly have read the letter correctly. There was no way that Cal would have gotten engaged to some woman she had never heard of when he had promised that he would marry her.

But did he really promise that? They were barely more than children at the time, spinning carelessly around the dance floor at their first ball when he told her that someday, they would be married. He mentioned it before he left for school. And then his letter came, and he said he would bring her home. She thought they had made plans together, and then he fell in love with someone without a word to her.

Stella closed her eyes. She felt like a fool.

She reached for her purse with trembling hands and pulled the letter out to reread it carefully. He never once mentioned marrying her. The two of them always referred to Chicago as home in their letters, but she had been so overwhelmed at the prospect of escaping her mother and a forced marriage that she didn't truly pay attention to what he had written to her. She had every intention to rip it to shreds when a knock startled her, and she hid the letter beneath her pillow as a reflex. Her mother couldn't know.

"Miss?" Jeanette's voice came from the other side of the door. "May I come in?"

Stella wiped frantically at her cheeks, forgetting that she was still wearing her gloves. The cotton barely helped to erase the tear tracks she knew had to trace down to her chin. When she called for Jeanette to come in, she hoped the girl wouldn't hear how her voice wavered.

Jeanette slid inside almost silently. With one look, Jeanette asked, "Are you alright, miss?"

No such luck.

"I'm fine." She glanced away.

Was Miss Castle graceful like Jeanette? Cal always teased Stella that she was all elbows and bones. Tall like a willow, sharp edges, and clumsy.

And, of course, he loved Miss Castle. He had only been Stella's friend. How could she be angry with him for betraying their understanding to marry the love of his life?

A handkerchief invaded her vision. "You've been crying, miss."

With a glare, she snatched the offending object away from Jeanette. She yanked her gloves off her hands and wiped angrily at her cheeks.

She hated him. She hated him so much.

"Miss?" Jeanette asked again, and Stella was struck with the urge to do something: yell, scream, rage, anything but feel so helpless. So pathetic. So desperate. She was nothing like those suffragists she always admired. But then the maid broke through the fog as she crouched before her, her voice gentle. "What happened?"

Reluctantly, Stella reached under her pillow and retrieved the letter, passing it to Jeanette. The girl's face paled; her mouth fell open. Her eyes darted to Stella, then back to the paper.

"That awful man!" the girl muttered under her breath.

"I'm a fool."

"No, miss." Jeanette reached for the handkerchief again.

She poured some water and dabbed at Stella's cheeks the way Stella once saw a mother do to her child after a particularly nasty fall. She had always been jealous of that child, of the comfort the girl received from her mother through the simple act. Stella's mother had never been the warmest of people, and her father had always been too oblivious of her and her siblings to notice if they needed care. "It could have happened to anyone."

"It could have," Stella muttered bitterly, her pride smarting as badly as her heart. "But I'm the one who fell for it." She brushed Jeanette's hands away. She wasn't a child. She shouldn't need to be comforted like one. "I don't want to go home."

She reached into her purse and pulled Cal's letter. Without thinking too much about what she was doing, she ripped it clean in half and then in half again.

"Please get rid of this." Even though she knew it was childish of her, she couldn't help but add, "If you would be so kind as to dispose of any future letters from him."

The maid hesitated before she took the scraps. "Yes, miss."

Jeanette moved to the door.

"Wait!" Stella called to her. Jeanette paused, turning slightly. "I have dinner tonight with Lord Pemberton. I'll need to get ready soon."

Jeanette nodded and left the room. The door closed behind her with a resounding click.

11

———————

WILLIAM

THERE WAS something different about Stella. Something had changed from that afternoon. The glow that had sparkled in her eyes since they met was gone.

Around them, waiters in stiff suits scurried between the tables, but she didn't seem to notice them anymore. Not the way she had that afternoon.

There was something somber about her appearance too. The dress she wore was nothing like the shining sapphire gown she had worn only a few nights before. Instead, it was as dark as the midnight sky, dotted with tiny silver beads like stars against the silken backdrop. Somehow, it looked like she was in mourning.

She had barely spared a glance at him. Not since he met her in the lobby. Not as they walked into the restaurant, nor as they sat down. Her eyes stayed on the menu as if she was afraid of what he would see there.

It didn't make sense. The woman he had come to know over the last few weeks was not afraid. She was bright and vibrant and full of life. She made him feel alive and feel things he didn't even know he wanted.

"You're quiet tonight," William said to try to get her attention. She didn't move, didn't present any indication that she
had heard him. He sighed and tried again. "Did something
happen?"

She didn't look up. "Just received a bit of bad news."

Her fingers worried at the edges of the menu. Whatever
news she received had delivered her a debilitating blow.

He lowered his menu and tried again to catch her eyes.
What could have possibly made her act like this? "Nothing
happened to your family, I hope."

She shook her head. "No, nothing like that."

He stared until she sighed and looked at him for the first
time all night. Her gaze only reached his chin, and he
wondered if she couldn't physically bring herself to look any
higher. Her teeth tugged at her lower lip as if to delay her
words.

"I found out Cal's been engaged to another woman the
entire time." Her eyes dropped again, focusing on her fingers.

William choked. What kind of idiot was this Cal? The
woman had to be spectacular for Cal to give up on the goddess
before him. All he managed to get out was, "That's
unexpected."

She looked up at him, finally, a bit wryly. "To say the least."

They fell into silence again, and William couldn't help but
feel a little sick. She was hurt, and he had no way to help her
feel better.

Bertie would have a laugh if he could see him now. But
Bertie would have known what to say to reassure her.

William swallowed. He was glad Bertie never actually met
her, else he might have lost her to his friend. They were more
alike, and a match between Bertie and Stella made a surprising
amount of sense in his mind. Both were outgoing and opinion-
ated. They looked to the future and paid very little attention to
traditions.

"Would you ever reconsider marrying me?" she asked suddenly, and William choked on his food. "I know you said you didn't want to, but—"

She wouldn't meet his eyes again, and he swallowed the lump of lamb in his throat.

"Why?" he asked before he could help himself. She hesitated, her lip between her teeth again. The movement drew his eyes to her mouth, and it took him a second longer than it should have to realize she wasn't going to answer. "I mean, why now?"

He cringed. He regretted the question nearly as soon as he had spoken it. He knew why now. Cal humiliated her and made her feel undesirable.

He was hardly her first choice.

"We've spent time together. We've gotten to know each other." She smiled at him, but it lacked the depth of emotion she displayed that afternoon. His stomach felt heavy. "The day we met, you came across as rather arrogant. And at the Exhibition, you drove me insane."

Her words should have been playful. If she had said them a few hours ago, they would have been. Now, they were flat. Lifeless.

He grimaced. "That wasn't my intention."

He had been annoyed. She was so enamored with someone else and hadn't planned on giving him a chance. He fooled himself earlier with the way she teased him and held onto him that she might have felt something, but now, he was only a consolation prize. And he was so desperate for her affection that he would take any scraps that he could get.

He was pathetic.

"I was hasty in my judgment of you," she admitted, and he had never hated her hands more. What was so fascinating about them that she kept looking at them? "I apologize for that." She sighed. It was the first real emotion she had shown all evening besides that cold blankness. "I'm realizing there's a lot of things I shouldn't have done. Being rude to you was one of them."

"If you were rude, so was I."

His rudeness had stemmed from a place of jealousy, but he saw now that there was no point in it. Her heart belonged to a man who had treated her like dirt. To be jealous felt too much like hope that things would change. They wouldn't.

"I think you might know me better than anyone." She played with her thumbnail. "You wouldn't try to change me."

That's what it came down to.

He looked down at his plate. The mint sauce sat in swirls on the dish. Food never seemed so unappetizing as it did in that moment.

It had nothing to do with love or caring. It had to do with the fact that he was the best of her bad options.

"It's rather unorthodox for you to ask me, but yes, I'll marry you."

He had always been a masochist. He would have never put up with his father's criticism if he wasn't. He wouldn't keep torturing himself with a woman who would never look at him half as lovingly as she had stared at that damn letter the day they met.

"Not just in theory?"

He had to keep himself from inhaling at the way her voice sounded. For a split second, he could almost believe that she could come to feel for him in that way.

"Not just in theory," he agreed. "I will marry you, Stella Craven."

He risked a glance up. From the way she looked at him, he could almost fool himself into thinking she cared. In a moment of weakness, he reached for her hand and kissed it. Inside, he felt only cold.

WILLIAM HAD SPENT months excited for the Olympics. He marked the different event dates on his calendar, cleared his schedule and obligations, and coordinated with Bertie to make sure he would have someone to commentate on the events with. But that day, he could barely summon the energy to care.

That morning, he tried to get ready, but the thoughts of facing Bertie with his news plagued him. He shuddered. After his mother's overzealous reaction, William didn't want to tell anyone. Being engaged didn't feel like a win. It felt like he was the silver medalist, wondering if he would ever be good enough to place gold.

He allowed his valet, Richard, to bully him into a light gray jacket and close his cuffs with the enamel cufflinks. They didn't feel enough like armor to satisfy him. He felt like he was heading into battle and needed to be properly suited.

When he repeated his thoughts to Richard, his valet snorted.

"Would you prefer chainmail, my lord?" The man tugged at the lapel until it lay flat. "Perhaps a sword?"

William rolled his eyes.

"As always, I knew I could count on you."

This time, Richard stayed silent, other than the knowing smirk.

"I'VE SECURED us absolutely capital seats for the discus throw."

The excitement in Bertie's voice was odd. For one, neither of them had ever watched discus. They both played cricket in school, and William still played in the annual match between the estate and the village.

"That's…" he hesitated, trying to figure out how not to offend his friend, "wonderful news."

Bertie laughed. "You don't have to pretend to be thrilled, Pem."

William shrugged. He didn't have an opinion either way on the sport. He was mostly there to try to keep his mind from the events of the night before.

"How did you even get these tickets?" The stadium was crowded, and it appeared that discus had quite the following. It seemed odd that such good seats were still available.

Bertie glanced away, shifting uncomfortably. "I won them in a card game."

"Who did you win them from that has you looking like that?"

"An investor." He sighed. "I felt dreadful taking them, but he insisted."

"You cheated, didn't you?" His question was met with a glare. It was just like Bertie to cheat at cards, so William wasn't even surprised. His friend spent their school days using his talents to swindle the older students into helping with his schoolwork and chores. It explained his guilty expression.

The tournament began, and they quieted. William heard someone behind them mention that forty-some people were competing. He wasn't sure what the great appeal was of watching people throw a metal disc, but he supposed that people could say that about any sport.

"Something's bothering you." Bertie's eyes burned into the side of his face though William pointedly stared at the field. "What happened?"

"I'm engaged."

His friend dropped his binoculars. The glass made an uncomfortable cracking sound as they hit the stands. "The girl from the races?"

He only nodded in response.

"But you seemed mad about her."

He shrugged. He didn't want anyone else to know the extent of his stupidity. He knew Miss Craven was using him, and he allowed it to go on like a fool.

Fortunately, Bertie seemed to understand that he didn't want to talk about it and turned back to the field.

He wondered what it meant at the end of the day that only the Americans won medals.

12
____

STELLA

THE ANCIENT DOWAGER Countess of Wraughtley was nothing like the current Countess. Lady Wraughtley—Lord Pemberton's mother, that was—had a presence that was hard to duplicate, something that drew people to be around her. The Dowager Countess made Stella feel inferior. Stella shifted under the woman's gaze. Everything about her and Pemberton House felt stifling.

The room was cluttered, garnished in heavy drapery and gaudy, uncomfortable furniture that was all the rage fifty years earlier. Knickknacks cluttered every surface, creating a claustrophobic fortress that surrounded them and threatened to bury them should they touch the wrong piece.

The Dowager Countess wore a stiff gown of many ruffles that looked more like the bustled garments of twenty years ago than the streamlined gowns Stella and her mother wore. Even the current Lady Wraughtley wore a slimmer silhouette than her mother-in-law. The day they arrived at Pemberton House, which served as the dower house, the Dowager Countess made many thinly veiled remarks before Lady Wraughtley left them to fend for themselves against the formidable old aristocrat.

When they first set foot inside the door of the house, Stella never expected to spend so long living with Lord Pemberton's grandmother. Like every day since they arrived, the Dowager Countess had claimed the middle of the sofa for herself, forcing Stella and her mother to sit in the short, clumsy Victorian chairs that Stella was sure were for decoration instead of sitting. That or the many layers of petticoats and bustles of the decades past had padded the derrière of the women who once sat in such chairs.

Stella shifted and attempted to find a more comfortable position.

"Sit up straight, young lady, and stop fidgeting," the woman snapped. Her accent was so thick that Stella could barely make out her words.

From the other chair, her mother glared at her, and Stella froze.

"In my day," the Dowager Countess continued, looking down her nose in a way that should have been impossible from her height and position, "no young lady would behave in such a way."

Stella swallowed and fought the urge to cower. "I apologize, Lady Wraughtley."

The woman scoffed dismissively. She eyed Stella the same way one might eye a bug they wanted to squish.

A maid with shaking hands set a tea service on the table, but Stella didn't dare move, even though she was dying of thirst.

The old lady thrust her nose into the air again and took no note of the maid ducking quickly from the room. "I do look forward to telling my grandson that you are a completely unsuitable bride."

Stella glanced out the window. The leaves on the trees outside had changed colors. Summer was over, but the weather didn't seem much cooler than it had been in June. The change in seasons only seemed to make the Dowager Countess more bitter.

"—missing so much of the wedding preparations. You clearly will be unable to keep up with the pressures of marriage and a peerage. I suspect that you'll be running back to America in a mere matter of months." Stella looked to her mother. She hadn't meant to drift off while the Dowager Countess was speaking, but she had no idea what the woman was talking about. "After all, Americans can't commit to anything."

Stella choked. Her mother wasn't doing much better. For all her talk of American impropriety, the Dowager Countess lacked any sort of filter from her thoughts to her mouth. Was her behavior because of her age, or had the woman always been so rude?

What color would the Dowager Countess turn if Stella told her that her tactlessness wasn't very British of her? There was no cunning, clever wording to hide her true meaning. Instead, she smacked everyone upside the head with her blunt statements.

It was amazing how many insults the Dowager Countess could think up about her. Stella's manners were atrocious. She was too thin to possibly bear children—heirs, the Dowager Countess had called them—and wouldn't she like to eat some more?

The nights they ate dinner at the manor were almost a relief, if only so the woman would have other targets.

Dinner that night wasn't the reprieve Stella hoped for. Her father-in-law-to-be hated her as much as his mother. He couldn't make it more obvious. Every pointed gaze and every invasive question told those in attendance he thought Stella was an unsuitable bride for his son. When Stella first made the mistake of asking a question about what to call Lady Wraughtley and the Dowager Countess while they sat at the same table, the Earl replied that "A British girl wouldn't have to ask. She would already know." It seemed to set the tone for all of their future encounters.

To make matters worse, Lord Pemberton refused to meet her eyes. She wasn't sure what she had done. Something had changed since they were engaged. She wished she knew what she had done.

The one highlight of dining at the manor was that Lady Margaret was actually rather pleasant. The girl was a year younger than Stella and had the sheltered sort of life one expected of a society girl. But she was also well-read and asked Stella many questions about living in the States. Lady Margaret was no replacement for Rebecca, but in time, Stella thought they might become good friends.

"THAT WAS AN UTTER DISASTER," her mother proclaimed as they entered their set of rooms at Pemberton House. It wouldn't have been proper for Stella to stay at the manor while she was engaged to Lord Pemberton. They might have gotten up to something nefarious. Like reading. Perhaps a little music.

She doubted it, though. Lord Pemberton claimed to have no musical talent.

Instead, they had spent months stuck at Pemberton House. Despite the spaciousness of the cottage, it never seemed like there was anywhere she could hide.

"It could have been worse."

Her mother turned on her. "How?"

How indeed? And she was voluntarily choosing to live with these people? People who acted like she was the scum of the earth?

But she cared for Lord Pemberton. For some odd reason, she wanted him to be happy, and she knew that would never happen so long as the threat of losing Wraughtley hung over his head. He had talked so passionately about the lands, about the tenants who relied on the family, and about the house that employed dozens of staff for centuries. Over the past few months, Stella realized that being a viscountess would put her in a position to change things. Instead of being just the socialite daughter of an upstart newspaperman, she could make a real difference, and that was all she'd truly wanted.

She just had to put her personal feelings aside. They didn't matter. Cal proved that.

"The Earl could have disinherited Lord Pemberton when he brought me here."

Her mother glared.

13

WILLIAM

RETURNING to Wraughtley did not bring the relief William hoped. In theory, he had everything he could have wanted. Miss Craven was going to marry him. Though they were not yet married, her inheritance already paid the income taxes and absorbed the costs from the tenants. They were going to be able to pay back the bank and keep Wraughtley. He should have felt happier.

Instead, he felt listless. His father was displeased with his choice of bride, despite the fact that she was nearly the only reason they had a roof over their heads. His grandmother was equally annoyed that Miss Craven and her mother had taken up residence in Pemberton House, his grandmother's home since his grandfather's death. It felt like everyone relied on him to fix things but complained about how he accomplished it.

To escape the craziness at the house—between the wedding preparations and the repairs that the house needed— he sought refuge in the stables. He sent one of the grooms, Charles, to saddle his horse, Apollo. Apollo was a gray Arabian who took his name from the Greek god of the sun and lived up to that name; William had never come across a horse who loved being in the bright sunlight more.

It would be nice to get away from his family for a few hours and the disapproving glares his father sported near constantly now. It was an unseasonably dry October, but that meant it was perfect weather for riding.

Charles no sooner finished with Apollo when Miss Craven walked into the stable. She wore a riding habit that reminded him of the midnight sky and the gown she wore on the best and worst night of his life. A hat shaded her face. She looked like she had stepped straight from one of the fashion plates that Margaret poured over.

"Do you mind if I join you?" she asked. A riding crop was in her hands.

He resisted the urge to shrug, to look away, to do anything but meet her eyes. He didn't want to know what he would see there. Instead, he took Apollo's reins from Charles. "Of course."

He nodded to the groom, who moved to prepare another horse.

"I think it's only fair to warn you," she spoke, her voice teasing, "I don't normally ride horses."

His mother mentioned something about that. But... he had thought... "My mother said that you did."

She drew closer but stopped when her skirts entered his vision. He looked up as she ran a leather-gloved hand along Apollo's back. She stared into the distance, a far-off look on her face.

"I drive cars. My brother has a roadster, and our aunt taught us how to drive."

He shuddered. "That seems dangerous."

She shook her head. "You could get thrown from a horse and break your neck. A car is no more dangerous."

He had to laugh at that. Charles led one of the more sedate

mares, a bay-colored Arabian whom William instantly recognized as Artemis, out into the center aisle. The groom had saddled Artemis with the side-saddle that his sister preferred. It fit well, even though Artemis wasn't Margaret's normal horse.

"Well, you don't have to worry about that. No one is going to break their neck today." He reached for the reins for the horse from Charles and led the mare closer. "This is Apollo and Artemis. Artemis is very gentle, and you'll have no problems with her." She reached her hand out to stroke the mare's nose, and William turned to Charles. "Help her mount."

With that, he mounted Apollo and let Charles worry about helping Miss Craven.

THEY RODE TOGETHER in a strange quiet across the grounds. For someone who said she didn't normally ride a horse, Miss Craven managed quite well.

He knew where he would like to take her in hopes that she might see the land as he did. One of the hills gave a spectacular view of the county. It overlooked both the village and the manor. The field surrounding it was overgrown with wildflowers, dotting the land with pink splotches like an Impressionistic painting.

When they reached the top of the hill, he dismounted and offered her a hand to climb down. She smiled, thanking him softly.

"Turn around," he ordered.

She inhaled sharply as she faced the village. Her eyes widened, and lips parted slightly. "It's stunning."

He pressed his lips together to keep himself from saying anything impulsive. It was easy to forget himself around her. It took him a moment to compose himself, to stop himself from telling her that she was stunning. He knew such comments would not be welcomed or appreciated. He doubted she noticed that he kept silent.

"This is one of my favorite spots."

A smile spread over her face. "I can see why." She glanced back at him. "Thank you for bringing me up here."

He nodded.

They stood in silence, watching the world go by. They were close enough that the wedding preparations could be seen. One end of the village had been overtaken by autumn flowers and bright ribbons. Though the wedding would not occur until December, the village seemed to be in a constant state of celebration.

"This is the first time we've been alone in weeks." Her words surprised him. He didn't think she wanted to spend time with him, especially not alone with him, so he hadn't tried to seek her out. He didn't want to force his presence on someone who saw this whole charade as some sort of consolation prize.

Half of the time, she walked around with a mask of indifference fixed on her face. She did a surprisingly good job at handling his grandmother, though, at least in front of him.

"We were in London before," he offered as an excuse rather than own up to the fact that he had been avoiding her on purpose. "My parents are more modern than my grandmother is." William ducked his head. He knew that the Dowager Countess was a trying sort. "I hope she hasn't been driving you too insane."

At that, she failed to contain her laughter, but it wasn't the happy sort. It was more bitter.

"She's only commented on my crass American personality," she muttered with a roll of her eyes, "and how I slouch as if I'm a farmhand." Suddenly, she shot him a grin, and her whole face lit up. "I don't even know how to slouch!"

"I'm sorry to hear that."

She shook her head. "I've heard worse."

The worst part was that she probably had. While most people never said what they thought about you to your face, most of them were more than happy to gossip about it behind your back. If you weren't well known in society, it was easy enough to gossip with someone who never knew who you were and find out everything that was being said about you. He had become well-known because of his courtesy title, but Bertie still had no problem walking right up to a woman and finding out everything that was being said about anyone.

"We can have lunch here," he offered suddenly.

Despite spending days avoiding her, now that he was alone with her, he didn't want to leave. It was stupid and irrational, and he hated that he felt like that.

She glanced at the horses, her eyebrows raised.

"Did you bring food?" She glanced in the direction of the manor. "Or is someone bringing it out?"

He could have hit himself.

"Neither. I didn't let anyone know." How could he? It was such a spur-of-the-moment idea. No one, not even the best of servants, could anticipate such a wild request when he hadn't spent any time with her since they had been back. Stuck with sudden inspiration, he turned back to his saddlebag and dug around.

He planned to snack while he was out there, so he had asked for something to tide him over until dinner. It wouldn't be elaborate like a picnic would have been. He had wanted to avoid everyone today and enjoy some quiet time to himself. It would be interesting to see what Richard packed for him.

A tin filled with cherries and biscuits—the latter of which had grown soggy from one of the cherries that had been pierced—and a canteen. He walked back to her and held up his meager supplies. "I found these."

She laughed, slipped her hand out of one of her gloves, and took a cherry off the top. "Thank you."

Watching her bite into the little fruit, the stem in between her fingers, was more mesmerizing than it should have been. What would her lips taste like right now? Would they be sweet from the juice? His mouth felt dry. He swallowed hard, but it made no difference. He unscrewed the canteen and took a gulp of the water, mostly to do something that didn't involve watching her.

"It's very beautiful here," she told him like he didn't know that.

He made a vague gesture, not wanting to repeat the mistake of looking at her again. "Everything here has been in my family for centuries."

"You're proud of it." He was taken aback by how fond her voice sounded, and he couldn't help but glance at her. A smile was on her face. It looked so similar to the one she had when they stood on his London rooftop that, for a moment, it was easy to forget months had passed since that night. A grin spread across his face before he could help it.

"Of course I am." The words fell out of his mouth, and she turned to look at him. He wanted to say something, anything, that would make her understand. Wraughtley was the most important thing in his life, was something worth preserving and protecting. "It's my legacy. I know that I'm only a caretaker of the estate, taking care of it for the next generation."

"What a heavy weight to bear."

He swallowed. "Perhaps. But it's one I've always accepted."

She glanced back at the horizon, and he could feel her slipping away again.

"It's not so bad," he tried again. He closed his eyes for a moment and licked his lips. This was important. It didn't matter if she never returned his feelings for her, whatever those feelings might be, so long as she didn't walk away. "The people that live here, in the village, are like family. They've lived here for as long as we have. So long as we own the land, no one can force them from their homes. What they grow and make goes towards the taxes to keep everything together."

"It's symbiotic," she muttered.

"What?"

She shook her head a little. "My little sister, for all that she pretends to be interested in nothing, is fascinated by biology." His brow furrowed. Stella had some interesting ideas about a woman's place in the world. "A symbiotic relationship is one that is mutually beneficial. In this case, they provide, and you provide in turn."

He blinked. He never thought about it that way. He only ever knew that they needed each other, and it was his duty to keep Wraughtley together.

"Why have things gotten so bad financially?"

He blinked. He supposed he should have expected she would ask at some point.

"A number of reasons. There have been some gambling issues in the past. We have land that hasn't been used in years. There have been several seasons of bad harvests, so the tenants haven't always been able to afford rent."

A frown overtook her face, though she didn't turn towards him. Other than her expression, there was no indication that she was actually listening to him.

"Do they have to make up the difference when they can afford it?"

"No." She stared at him, eyes wide. "I'm limited in what I can actually do right now. My father holds power over anything involving the estate."

She grimaced.

"I plan to change that," he assured her, "when I'm the earl."

The way she looked at him made him want to shift under

her gaze. It was like she could see something that he was missing. He swallowed again.

Realization washed over him. His father wasn't old, not compared to other family members. His grandmother was eighty-seven, while his father would be sixty-three in another month. They could be bankrupt before his father did anything to correct the problems, years of draining whatever inheritance that Stella brought.

He scrubbed a hand across his face and grimaced. "I don't know what to do," he admitted. "I've tried convincing him for years that things need to change, but he never wants to listen. Every time I say anything, I'm automatically wrong. He doesn't even have to say it. It's just implied. He's just so stubborn."

He all but spat the last word. She stared at him, looking a little surprised by his outburst. Then, the expression vanished from her face as she replaced it with something that made him almost feel warm inside. A small smile crossed her face.

"We'll figure something out."

For a second, he could almost believe they were a team instead of two people forced into this situation together. A smile made its way onto his lips before he could stop it.

She turned back at the fields, a wistful look on her face, and the moment was over. He wasn't willing to delude himself into thinking she had any sort of feelings for him.

"I hope you'll enjoy living here," he said softly.

"I think I could be happy here."

He wanted to believe she meant she could be happy with him but wasn't willing to give in to that fantasy. Nothing but heartache could come from it.

She turned and walked towards her horse. She gently ran her hand down Artemis' snout. "I'll race you back to the stables."

She mounted so smoothly that he was left gaping. It had taken Margaret ages to get onto her saddle without looking like a fool, and she still couldn't get on it without help. Miss Craven said she didn't really ride horses, but no amateur was so comfortable that she would be able to ride like that.

"You lied!" he realized.

"Hardly!" she called over her shoulder, a smirk on her face. "It's just like riding a bicycle."

He blinked at her words as she disappeared down the hillside. She mentioned a race. He wouldn't let her win.

14

———————

WILLIAM

DINNER THAT NIGHT was the same it had been since they had come back to Wraughtley. The only change was that Bertie was there for the wedding, arriving far earlier than anyone—except maybe his mother—expected. It was always strange to him that the Countess was friendly with his boyhood friend. The two had nothing in common other than Bertie flattered her, and his mother loved to be flattered.

"We're so glad you were able to get away," his mother said as the footman slid near invisibly between them with trays of food.

"I'm glad you invited me." William stopped himself from staring, but just barely. "Lancashire always feels so dreary this time of year."

William knew better than anyone that Bertie wasn't actually referring to the climate. He was talking about the fact that every year since his sisters first presented in court, they came back from London more disappointed and despondent than the year before. The grandchildren of a baron had no real leg up in society. None of them had titles, and the girls' dowries were next to nothing, as their father had married for love over money. He imagined they probably gave Bertie grief about William's choice to marry an American woman when there were so many eligible young British ladies looking to advance themselves. But Bertie never wanted to tie himself to any of them.

"Of course." His mother smiled warmly. "You're always welcome here."

William glanced at Stella. He wondered if she felt welcome. She didn't look particularly comfortable. He wished he could do something to draw her out of the darkness that seemed to haunt her. It had been that way ever since *that* night, but it got worse since they arrived in Wraughtley. Being around his grandmother constantly surely didn't help, and from what little he knew about his mother-in-law-to-be, the woman seemed like she could give his grandmother a run for her money. Even their ride was only a temporary reprieve for Stella.

Next to him, his sister spoke, eyes shining brightly. "William said earlier that you drove all the way here."

Bertie grinned, and William barely could stop himself from letting his head fall into his hands. The thought of his best man driving across the country by himself rather than being sensible and taking the train or allowing a chauffeur to bring him was disturbing.

"By yourself?" Of course that was the part his grandmother picked up on. She stared at Bertie like he was something to be cleansed from her house. Nearly twenty years since William's grandfather died and she still thought of Wraughtley Hall as her domain.

Bertie's grin disappeared from his face, his eyes dropping to his dishes like a child being scolded. William knew the other man better than to believe he was being earnest. "Yes, Lady Wraughtley."

"Good Heavens!" Grandmother exclaimed and clasped her

hand over her heart in a way she often did when something didn't please her. "What is this world coming to?"

From the head of the table, his father groaned. "Mother…"

His grandmother glared at Father before turning back on Bertie. "Whatever do you pay a chauffeur for?"

Bertie chuckled.

"Well, I think it's marvelous."

Matching glares shot across the table at Stella from his grandmother and Mrs. Craven. "Of course you do," Grandmother said, eyes narrowed into slits. "You're American."

Stella ignored both of them. "In fact, I've placed an order for a Simplex."

A what?

"Stella!" her mother's sharp admonishment came.

"But who will drive it?" his grandmother asked.

"I will." She seemed so proud of it that he couldn't help but remember her earlier declaration about driving cars. But what on Earth did she need a car for? It wasn't like she needed to drive great distances to other cities. Could women even get driver's licenses?

"Whatever for?"

Stella smiled sweetly at his grandmother, and dread washed over him. "Because I'm a classless American."

To his left, his mother dropped her fork. It clanged noisily on her plate. His father choked on the sip of wine he had just taken. Mrs. Craven turned puce. Her eyes bulged from her head. His grandmother lost all color in her face.

"Bloody hell, Mother!" his father swore as he took another drink. "Did you really say that?"

His grandmother stared at Father, looking more like she was chastising a child than an Earl. "I have said a great many things in my life. You too will find that to be the case when you reach my age."

He felt Bertie's eyes on him, but William refused to look at him. His friend probably expected him to say something, perhaps to defend Stella's honor. But he was no knight, and she didn't seem like she had any trouble defending herself from his grandmother. William sighed. "Well, I, for one, do not understand the appeal of automobiles."

She smiled at him. "That is because one must be modern to appreciate it."

"If to be modern is to have no taste…"

"On the contrary. To be modern is to want more from life than to be shackled for all eternity." Those last words were spoken to her mother. Mrs. Craven looked moments away from popping a blood vessel.

"I'd love to ride in one before I decide," Margaret declared. Mother turned her head sharply.

"If it's alright," Bertie said like he was actually seeking permission, "I can take you out in it tomorrow."

"That would be lovely. Thank you, Bertie."

His sister beamed, her cheeks flushed, and William felt a little foolish that he never saw it before. How could he have missed it? Had he really been so caught up in his own problems to miss that his sister had developed feelings for Bertie, of all people?

Not that there was anything wrong with Bertie. Margaret was his sister, and he wanted whatever was best for her. The idea of her having a relationship with Bertie was just strange.

His grandmother's knife and fork barely clinked as she set them down on her plate, but they rang out like a gong banging noisily at the end of the table. "And now my appetite has been successfully killed."

William swallowed. So she saw it too?

He glanced across the table at Stella, but his fiancée was too busy looking between his sister and his friend thoughtfully.

His grandmother stood, and all attention fell to her. The

decorative cane shook in her hand, betraying her rage. His father set down his silverware, and everyone else followed.

"Right," his mother said, desperately trying to regain some measure of control over the situation. "Shall we adjourn to the drawing room?"

A FEW DAYS LATER, William found himself bent over the desk in the library. Mr. Walker, the milkman, asked for an extension on his rent for the month after one of his cows died unexpectedly, and he'd been unable to fill all of his deliveries. Mr. and Mrs. Davies, the owners of the apothecary, were both ill, and neither was able to work. There were dozens of other excuses. It never got easier hearing it or trying to tell them that they had to pay in order to stay.

A headache blossomed behind his eyes, and he pinched his nose in a desperate attempt to stave it off. It was clear that was a pointless hope.

Bertie strolled in whistling, the noise piercing his ears. William eyed the letter opener on the desk and wondered if it would be ill-advised to stab the other man.

"Would you please stop?"

"Why? It's a beautiful day. Sun shining. Bird chirping. You should come enjoy the fresh air."

William turned and glared at his friend. "I wish everyone would be less concerned with how I spend my days."

Bertie sat on the sofa and threw his arm over the back like he didn't have a care in the world. William envied him. When Bertie spoke, his tone was light and free. "We worry because we care."

It was at that moment that Stella came into the library. She smiled at them both but otherwise didn't say a thing. He vaguely knew that she was supposed to be looking at food options or something with his mother, not reading a book. It took him a moment or two longer than he would admit to realize Mother had come up with an excuse that allowed Stella away from her mother and his grandmother without anyone getting angry.

"Good day, Miss Craven," Bertie greeted, tipping an invisible hat to her.

Her smile brightened, and he hated that it was directed at Bertie. "Good day, Mr. Rutledge."

"Bertie, I insist."

"In that case, please call me Stella."

"Perhaps you would like to join Lady Margaret and me on that drive now?"

"That would be lovely."

"And perhaps I'll even let you drive." She grinned. "Now, if only you could convince this one that all work and no play makes Jack a dull boy."

It was almost worth Bertie's needling to hear Stella laugh. She turned that smile on him, and he wondered if he'd be able to coax it out of her without Bertie's help. Probably not, he thought glumly.

"It's a lovely day," she said softly, their eyes meeting. "Won't you join us?"

His breath caught in his throat, and he nodded. How could he possibly say no to an invitation like that?

He expected her to look away, but she didn't. He barely heard Bertie muttering something about getting the car, and he darted from the room.

"Should I be worried?" he asked, his voice half-teasing. "If you're going to be driving?"

She rolled her eyes and laughed, stepping closer until she was a hair's breadth away from him. If he was to stand, their noses would be mere inches apart.

"I'll have you know that I'm an excellent driver."

He couldn't help but smile at that. "I suppose we'll see shortly."

She breathed in. In that second, they were the only two people in the world. He didn't want that to end, but then something flashed across her face, and she stepped back. "We should go."

"Of course."

She turned and strode quickly from the library. Her skirts swished in her wake. He swallowed a groan of frustration. It felt like every time he took a step forward, he took several steps back.

WILLIAM JOINED the others in the front of the house. Bertie's shiny black car waited there. Bertie wore an interesting outfit consisting of a long tan duster, a scarf, a leather cap and gloves, and goggles that made him look bug-eyed. Stella wore something similar, though her hat wasn't nearly as tight and had a sort of veil that seemed like it would protect her face.

William hadn't realized riding in an automobile required special clothing besides a duster. From Margaret's helpless expression, she hadn't realized either. Hopefully, his glasses would be all the eye protection he needed.

"She's a beauty, isn't she?" Bertie said, slapping William on the back. "I just had her shipped in from America. Did you know they're starting to mass produce these?"

No, and he hadn't cared to know. The whole thing seemed like a ridiculous passing fad for the terribly wealthy. In a few years, they would be onto the next thing. Perhaps those flying machines.

"My brother wanted to buy stock in Ford." Stella circled the vehicle and eyed it appreciatively. "Mother thought it would be a phase and convinced him otherwise." Bertie laughed. "How does it drive?"

"Like a dream."

Inside, William seethed, but he fought to keep his face passive. It wasn't hard to see how interested Stella was in the car or that Bertie was flirting with his fiancée. Beside him, Margaret swallowed audibly as she stared at the contraption.

Stella was a demon behind the steering wheel, though a little discomfort was worth it to see her so carefree. Well, that's what he told himself as he held on tightly. *Was it possible to be thrown from a vehicle when it moved like that?*

The car slid around the corner on the dirt road. Dust kicked up in their wake. William choked and wished he had brought a scarf to shield his mouth. The car slowed to a stop as she lifted her goggles.

"That was brilliant!" Bertie shouted from the front.

William blinked several times to clear the dirt from his eyes. Beside him, his sister clung to the seat. "You actually enjoy that?"

"Of course." Bertie shot a bright grin in Margaret's direction.

William was somewhere between those two on the scale of how much he enjoyed it.

"Perhaps we ought to switch," Stella suggested. "Save poor Lady Margaret's delicate sensibilities."

Margaret straightened, bristling at Stella's words. "I'm not delicate. Man was just not meant to go that fast!"

Stella smiled a bit wistfully. "My Simplex will go much faster. Vanderbilt got his over ninety miles an hour a few years ago, and mine's a newer model."

"I think I will never be riding with you."

Bertie chuckled, slid out of the car, and opened the boot. He held up a picnic basket like it was some sort of trophy. "Lunch, anyone?"

15

STELLA

THE NEXT MORNING, Lord Pemberton showed up at the door of Pemberton House before breakfast was finished. Stella felt a thrill of satisfaction at the reactions of her mother and the Dowager Countess. The annoyance on their faces was as clear as day. During breakfast, the Dowager Countess announced that they would be looking at linens for the wedding lunch. How dare he interrupt wedding preparations?

Not that her or Lord Pemberton's opinion mattered for any of it, she thought. Most of the preparations consisted of her mother attempting to take control and the Dowager Countess telling her mother that the bride's family had no place in planning the wedding. About the only thing they both had agreed on was that the wedding would take place in the afternoon.

The Dowager Countess quickly rejected Mother's idea of a tea before the day of the wedding where they thanked those who sent presents.

"What a tasteless American custom," the woman said when Mother first brought it up. Stella had attended a few of such parties hosted by her friends, and silently, she agreed with the Dowager Countess, not that she would ever admit it out loud.

Jeanette pinned her hat and handed Stella her gloves and sunshade. The sun had yet to peek through the clouds, leaving the morning cooler than usual. For that, Stella was thankful. She didn't think there was a better day to escape into the world outside Pemberton House.

Stella never thought she needed saving, but, in that moment, she was glad Lord Pemberton was there nonetheless.

"You're going alone?" Disgust painted the Dowager Countess' face clear for the world to see. "No chaperones?"

Actually, Stella was surprised her mother agreed to let her out of the house with so little of a fight. Perhaps Mother thought that Lord Pemberton wouldn't have any possible way to back out of the marriage after a day spent alone.

Not that he would. He needed her. He needed her money to save his estate, something that was clearly very important to him.

"Margaret's just outside," Lord Pemberton told her.

Lady Margaret didn't count as far as a chaperone went. She wasn't married, nor was she old enough to be considered a chaperone.

The Dowager Countess's cane shook slightly. "And she couldn't come in?"

"Sorry, Grandmama," Lady Margaret said, a little breathless as she stepped in the front door. "Miss Carr's cat had kittens!"

She held up a tiny orange scruff of fur. The creature sported a green satin ribbon around its neck.

If possible, the Dowager Countess' mouth puckered tighter, making her look even more like she had bitten a lemon wedge.

"This one's going to be mine when they're old enough." The kitten gave a yawn and snuggled into Lady Margaret's hands. Stella had to admit that the sight was adorable.

"We should probably be going," Lord Pemberton said. "Lots to do."

He smiled at his grandmother. They said goodbye as Stella escaped from the house before anyone could say otherwise. A moment later, Lord Pemberton and Lady Margaret followed and closed the door solidly behind them.

They strolled down the road, heading towards the village. Pemberton House was a decent walk from the little village, enough to separate the Dowager Countess from the hard-working people. The brisk morning air made it the perfect day for a walk. Stella didn't see a car nor horses waiting outside, so she wondered if they had walked from Wraughtley Hall to get there.

Once they were free from her mother's and the Dowager Countess' prying eyes, Lady Margaret turned to them. "I should probably get this little one back to her mother."

Lady Margaret stroked the kitten's head. Tufts of fur stuck up between her fingers. The tiny creature purred softly. With a smile, she sped her pace and walked into the dress shop.

Stella turned to Lord Pemberton as they walked through the village toward the farmland.

"Why is Pemberton House so close to Wraughtley Hall?" she asked. She had wondered about that for a while.

"Wraughtley used to be divided and governed by several viscounties and baronies. When this was only a viscounty, the area was ruled by multiple people, and Pemberton House was the lord's manor." He motioned around them. "The village is actually called Pemberton."

Stella blinked. She vaguely recalled that. She never really thought about it, though. Did that mean that Pemberton was his village and all of Wraughtley was his father's? Maybe it was like the difference between a mayor of a town and the governor of a state. It was probably a flawed analogy, but she knew she would understand better after she lived there for a while and had a chance to learn.

16

WILLIAM

"GOOD MORNING, MY LORD," a voice came as they walked down the road in the same direction that Margaret had gone. William turned to see who had spoken.

Gregory Townsend came closer, carrying his work tools. He could fix anything and could build anything. He was precisely the kind of man who could make anyone feel good about themselves. Something about his personality was always so bright, warm, and welcoming like sunshine. He didn't have much, but he never missed a rent payment.

He was something of a local fixture. William had no idea if the man was forty or eighty, but he had lived in the same house for as long as William could remember and never seemed to age. He'd always had gray hair and bright blue eyes. Since William was a boy, the village children knew Mr. Townsend as "Father Christmas." Every year, he dressed in a green coat and delivered little treats around the village.

It was pure luck Mr. Townsend would be the first person he introduced Stella to in the village, but he couldn't have chosen anyone better.

"Good morning, Mr. Townsend. Miss Craven, have you met Mr. Townsend?"

She shook her head as the man took off his hat.

"It's nice to meet you, Mr. Townsend." When Stella smiled at the man, it didn't look forced. For that, William was glad.

"A pleasure to meet you, Miss Craven."

Stella smiled. "Thank you."

He smiled before he turned back to William. "Is there anything I can do for you, my lord?"

William shook his head. "Not today. I thought Miss Craven would like to see some of Pemberton before the wedding."

Mr. Townsend reached into his basket, pulled out two myrtle flowers, and offered one to each of them. William vaguely remembered it meaning something about good luck but was more impressed that they hadn't been crushed by the tools.

Stella blushed as she took it. The blood turned her cheeks a pleasant shade of pink.

"Thank you," she whispered softly. Her eyes darted to William, but she quickly looked away rather than meet his gaze.

His stomach turned.

"William!" his sister called, and he forced his thoughts down. He didn't want to dwell on it.

"I should let you go, my lord. Miss Craven." Mr. Townsend bowed his head and backed away.

"Of course. Have a good day," he muttered, his mind still on the flower. Why had something so simple made her react that way?

"William," Margaret called again. "You can't keep Stella to yourself all day."

He looked at his sister. She stood on the stairs of the town's only clothing shop. She motioned to them, holding the kitten with her other hand.

Everyone in town knew that there were few things that Margaret adored more than tiny baby animals. She had once convinced Father to let her keep a baby goat and snuck it upstairs into the nursery. The goat got loose, found its way into the library, and ate some of Father's papers.

"Shall we?" he asked.

Stella startled and looked up from the myrtle, her expression almost guilty.

"Oh, yes."

She tucked the flower into her hat and walked beside him to the dress shop. Margaret, thankfully, stopped waving.

Miss Austin and Miss Carr, the proprietresses of the shop, loved Stella. She ordered a new pair of lace gloves, which made both of the women even happier, before joining Margaret in cooing over the kittens. Miss Carr's cat and the kittens were corralled into an area away from the fabrics on the shelves. He could only imagine the disaster the cats getting into them would cause.

"Do you think Miss Craven would like one, my lord?" Miss Carr asked him.

Stella had picked up a tiny one with gray fur that bordered on black from where it had wandered away from its mother. It was the only one that color. All of its siblings were shades of orange. There was something a little sad about it. He watched as she ran her fingers across its forehead, and it made a noise, sounding more like a baby bird than a cat.

"Perhaps." He honestly didn't know. They hadn't talked about the future or children or animals. He assumed that she would want children, and he knew their parents both expected them to have an heir.

She seemed content to run her fingertips through the kitten's fur. A small smile graced her face. He hated to ruin that with talk of the future.

"I know Lady Margaret has put a claim on at least one.

She hasn't happened to claim the one Miss Craven is holding, has she?"

Miss Carr smiled and shook her head. "No, my lord."

Margaret came up to him, having finally torn herself from the kittens. "If it's alright with you, I think I'll stay here a little while longer. You can go without me."

"Of course."

He'd never dream of getting between Margaret and a small animal. It didn't mean he wanted to watch her play with the litter all day.

Stella glanced at him and straightened, setting the tiny cat on the floor. It wandered over to the others but stayed on the outside, almost afraid of them. He felt sorry for it.

"It was lovely meeting you both," Stella told Miss Carr and Miss Austin.

"Thank you, Miss Craven," Miss Austin said in that prim way of hers. The woman was only a few years older than him, but he always thought she would have made a good school mistress if for no other reason than her ability to strike fear into the hearts of others. It was lucky that she had the sociable Miss Carr to interact with customers.

As they left the shop, he thought he saw Miss Carr tie a blue ribbon around the gray cat's neck.

Most people were working. He didn't want to interrupt the ones who weren't in shops, but he did plan on collecting rent from anyone who was due. He didn't want to put it off until they were in the thick of wedding preparations, and if William didn't do it, he knew his father wouldn't collect at all. At least, being as money-conscious as she was, Stella would appreciate the task.

"Where are we heading next?" she asked as they left the shop.

He pointed to the last house in the village. "That's Mr. Lipman's house."

The house was the late Mrs. Lipman's before they had gotten married, or so he had been told. Mr. Lipman had moved into it rather than live in the tiny one-room living space in the barn on his farmland. Since his wife's passing, nothing seemed to be right with the house and often was behind on the rent because of it. Every spring, the roof leaked. In the winter, drafts appeared out of nowhere. He often claimed it was haunted, but Mr. Townsend always fixed the roof and the drafts. William often wondered if the grouchy old farmer claimed something was wrong just to get some company. William wouldn't have been surprised.

The old farmer was utterly charmed by Stella and paid the rent without protest or excuses. It appeared she could put on a good show for others when she wanted. He wondered if that made him special somehow, that she hadn't tried after that first meeting. Or perhaps it was because of that first meeting.

Bringing Stella out with him to the village turned out to be a great idea. It was the smoothest day he ever had asking people for their payments.

"Your help was invaluable today. We made a great team." A delicate blush spread across her cheeks.

"I'm glad. Thank you for bringing me with you today."

"Everyone liked you."

"I liked them too. I've never spent much time around non-society people." She cringed. "That sounds awful, now that I'm saying it aloud. Mother never liked us socializing outside of our class, as if word would somehow get back to the other society ladies and it would taint our reputation." She glanced up at the sky. "Everything was so controlled. I was sent to the best finishing school that Mother could find, was told who I could talk to there, who I was supposed to avoid. When I was home, I had to be seen with the *right* people. Going out like this, talking to regular working people would have been a sin to her."

She fell quiet.

"May I ask you something?" he asked as they wandered toward Wraughtley Hall again. They were on the far side now, having collected the last of the farmers' rent, quite a walk from the village. He would have his driver bring her back to Pemberton House when they reached the Hall.

"Yes?"

"Why did the flowers Mr. Townsend give us upset you?"

She shook her head. "It didn't upset me."

She was lying. He knew it from the way she refused to meet his eyes. He sighed.

"Would you like one of Miss Carr's kittens?" They stepped onto the worn path between the forest and Wraughtley's gardens. Wraughtley Hall would soon be in sight. "Perhaps the gray one that you seemed fond of?"

She blinked. "Would you mind?" He shook his head. "He was such a sweet little thing."

The tiny cat had seemed rather sweet. And it would make her happy.

It had to be then that the skies opened. The icy rain soaked their clothes, and Stella shrieked, gathering her skirt as she ran, darting towards the only covering that was in sight. He did the only sensible thing and followed her. They took shelter under the Palladian bridge that crossed the pond behind the house.

"I didn't think it would rain today," he muttered. It hadn't fit into his plans for the day. It actually disrupted everything.

"Does anyone know when it'll rain?" Stella asked as she reached up and blindly felt around her hat. She pulled at something—a long pin—and the hat came off. The flowers on it looked ruined, or at least they did to him. What did he know about ladies' hats?

He glanced out at the sky. "I don't think it's going to let up anytime soon."

William sighed and pulled off his jacket. It figured that he tried to do something to help her feel like she belonged at Pemberton, and it backfired.

"I'm sorry," he said, his mood as gray as the clouds. "I wouldn't have suggested today if I had known."

Stella shot him a look, amused and almost—*dare he hope*—fond. "You don't control the weather."

She glanced at her hat, running her fingers through the flowers. Mr. Townsend's myrtle fell loose, and she clenched the fingers holding the hat.

"Will you tell me why you keep looking at that flower like it offended you?" he asked. He knew it was a foolish wish. She'd already denied that it bothered her.

"I was always told that myrtles were a wish for love in marriage."

He kept quiet. What could he say about that? There wasn't really anything he could say that wouldn't push her further away. It figured. He felt like any progress they had made until that minute faded away.

He swallowed and summoned up his courage. "I'd always heard that they meant luck."

A small smile crossed her face as she lifted her head, a distant look in her eyes. "Some luck would be nice."

The rain slowed to a drizzle. It seemed like they found some luck after all.

17

STELLA

IT WAS strange to be back in London after staying in Wraughtley. Stella supposed she had gotten used to the quiet of the countryside. Originally, London didn't seem noisier than Chicago, but at that moment, she wished she could cover her ears to block it all out.

Her mother led them to a fashion house that appeared to be a copy of the ones in France. The sign on the building declared it was "House of Dumont."

Inside, a grand, gilded mirror dominated one of the walls. Plush sofas surrounded the dressing area, and where, Stella assumed, house models would show off various clothes for them.

Today was the first time she could remember not being excited to shop. A sick feeling had embedded itself in the pit of her stomach and refused to leave no matter what she did.

An older woman, whom Stella assumed was Madame Dumont, stood flanked by two assistants. The older woman wore a gaudy dress, covered in lace and bobbles. It reminded Stella vaguely of the latest French fashions if she squinted and turned her head at an angle. Maybe it was copied from a blurry fashion plate. The assistants were dressed much more tastefully in simple gowns. Stella assumed it helped keep attention on Madame Dumont. If that was the intent, it worked.

"Welcome, Madame Craven." The woman spoke with an exaggerated French accent. "And this must be Mademoiselle Craven. Congratulations on your upcoming nuptials."

Her stomach turned, but Stella forced a smile onto her face and hoped she sounded sufficiently gracious as she said, "Thank you."

The woman beamed. "Your mother selected a gown that she thinks will be très chic for your wedding."

The French words only served to make Stella doubt the woman more. Out of the corner of her eye, her mother smirked. She looked like a cat who had gotten the cream.

"Stella is very excited to try it on," her mother said to the woman. Stella did her best not to react. She wasn't excited to try it on. Most girls dreamed of their wedding day. The dress, the flowers, the grandeur. She just wanted to get it over with.

It wasn't that marrying Lord Pemberton would be the worst thing. However, everything leading up to the wedding seemed so forced. Despite knowing that Lord Pemberton was only marrying her for her money, she enjoyed his company. But the wedding would be just another reminder that he didn't love her.

She shook her head slightly to clear it.

"Mademoiselle Craven," Madame Dumont said, "if you will please follow my assistant."

Stella nodded and walked forward. Jeanette followed. The assistant led them to the changing room and pushed the door open.

"Please let me know if you need any assistance."

"Thank you."

The woman smiled and closed the door behind them. Immediately, Jeanette started unfastening and unlacing Stella's dress. The underclothes would stay on, Stella supposed, only because it would be too much work to change them out in the shop. They had to make sure her trousseau fit, that her wedding gown fit. The underthings could wait.

"You've been quiet since the beginning of this." Stella kept her voice low so no one outside the door would hear them. She wanted someone to tell her she was doing the wrong thing, that marrying a man she had met only a few months ago was insane. She wanted Jeanette to tell her it was alright not to marry at all.

Instead, the girl merely inclined her head. "I apologize, miss. I don't have much to say."

Stella resisted the urge to roll her eyes. She knew Jeanette better than to think she didn't have an opinion. "You always have something to say."

The maid pressed her lips together until they formed a pale, narrow line. "I think, in this case, my opinions are best kept to myself."

She closed her eyes for a minute in an attempt to escape the judgement she saw written plain as day on Jeanette's face, but it didn't work.

Someone knocked on the door, and one of the assistants stepped inside, carrying a long ivory gown. Stella eyed the beading and lacework that must have taken days. The frills and baubles looked like they were waiting to be cut from the gown.

She stayed silent. A normal bride might have gushed over the dress and fussed about the lace, the coloring, and the way it looked on. She would have been excited because this was the moment she dreamed about since she was a little girl, second only to walking down the aisle and saying, "I do."

Stella was not a normal bride. The sight of the dress made her heart beat a little faster, but she didn't feel anything more for it than she did any other item of clothing, except resentment that she had not picked out the dress herself.

The collar felt high enough to choke her. The lace and ruffles tickled just under her chin. The sleeves were so tight it felt like she was wearing a straitjacket.

Everything about the dress was wrong.

The assistant pinned the veil on her head, and when Stella reached up, she felt a waxy, flowery headpiece.

"This has to be altered," she said, more to herself than to anyone.

"Miss?"

"The Countess asked that I wear the family tiara."

The girl's lips parted, her eyes going a little glossy as if she was upset at that, but for the life of her, Stella couldn't think why she would be.

"Of course, miss." The girl reached up to unpin the veil. Strands of hair came loose and fell in her face.

Jeanette brushed the fallen curls back into place. Stella wondered if the shop had another veil that they would put on her. It would be something as equally awful as the dress.

The assistant opened the door to the changing room. Jeanette bundled the train into her arms as they walked out, and the other assistant rushed forward to help Jeanette fan out the heavy train behind her like she was about to be presented to the King and Queen of England. Each step she took felt like she was heading to her own execution.

In the background of the salon, she heard Madame Dumont exclaim, "Ah! Magnificent, no?"

"Oh, yes! You do stunning work," her mother responded as Stella stopped in front of the mirror. Her mother stood and circled her. "The coloring is perfect, and it fits her so well."

Stella resisted the urge to close her eyes, refusing to look at herself in the mirror. She felt like a piece of art on display, a statue being appraised. Fashion was never supposed to feel that way.

"It suits her very well," Madame Dumont continued. "You chose well, Madame."

Stella glanced down at the mirror, and it took everything in her to not let her emotions show or her jaw drop in horror. If she started to cry now, she didn't think she would be able to stop. The dress was perfectly awful, the most hideous thing she'd ever seen. Madame Dumont and her assistants clearly took every scrap of lace, bauble, and button they could find and stitched it onto the dress.

Stella could not get married in that dress.

After her mother contemplated the dress for an appropriate amount of time, Stella was finally allowed to change back into her clothes. Her simple clothes followed a fashionable silhouette and not whatever shape that monstrosity was.

As soon as the door closed behind the assistant who removed that atrocity, Jeanette turned on her. "You've been quiet, miss."

Stella ignored her to focus on a spot on the wall before she started crying.

Jeanette's voice dropped lower, clearly afraid of being overheard. "You hated that awful gown."

A sob broke free from her lips before she could stifle it, and she quickly covered her mouth with her hand.

"I do hate it! It's terrible. I never would have chosen it." She fixed her gaze on the other girl, knowing she would understand. "I'd rather have bought a dress prêt-à-porter."

"Then why did you not say something?" Stella glared at her, and Jeanette cowered under the look.

"You know why. This isn't my wedding any more than it is Lord Pemberton's."

A handkerchief appeared before her, and she took it, scrubbing at her eyes. She didn't care if they turned red. She just wanted this whole awful extravagant show to be over with.

"We're just dolls in this whole affair," she whispered, "being told how to dress, how to walk."

She sniffled as she tried to collect herself. Out of the corner of her eye, Jeanette's hand lifted to her back, but she dropped it before it made contact.

Stella straightened up, glancing back at the maid.

"Not a word of this to anyone," she warned.

"Never, Miss."

THEY WALKED out of the shop, but Stella didn't feel like they had resolved anything. The dresses in the shop windows along the road looked nicer than her wedding gown. It would be altered slightly to better fit her and sent to Pemberton House. She wondered if Jeanette could intercept it before her mother knew it arrived. Perhaps she should do it herself to give the other girl some level of deniability. After all, Jeanette couldn't tell Mrs. Craven that the outrageously expensive dress had shown up before it went missing if she never knew the dress reached the house in the first place.

"I am so glad that I will see you settled before I return home."

Since winter was settling in, her family planned to stay until spring came before traveling back across The Atlantic. It would be her sister Effie's first extended trip abroad.

"Of course, Mother," Stella said agreeably, despite the fact that mentally, she was plotting the ghastly gown's demise.

"Your father will be arriving any day, as will Ambrose and Euphemia."

Stella knew as much. In fact, it was only due to Father's work schedule that they postponed their crossing until a mere two weeks before the wedding and risked it being too perilous and icy to make the trip. Father's business was far more important to him than attending his eldest daughter's wedding. Effie sent a telegram before they boarded in New York.

Did her mother know how demeaning it was when she called her second daughter by her full name rather than her chosen name? She wasn't the only target of her mother's attacks, but Effie would face them alone in the future.

"I'm looking forward to seeing them."

Her mother paused at the corner where a taxi waited for passengers. Jeanette rushed forward to open the door for them. For the first time in a long time, her mother smiled at her, but Stella found no satisfaction from it. "I'm proud of you, Stella. You're being very mature about this."

She stayed silent. Anything she said at that moment would likely cause a fight, and that was the last thing she wanted to do.

"I'm glad that you came around," her mother said as she stepped up into the cab.

Before Stella could follow her in, Jeanette caught her eyes. The look in them told her exactly how disappointed the other girl was in her. For some reason, Jeanette's disapproval weighed heavier on her shoulders than her mother's pride could lift them.

18

STELLA

THE PARLOR CAR was nearly empty, but her mother opted to find an empty compartment to rest in. Two old men played chess at one of the far tables. The one with less gray in his hair appeared to be losing horrendously, but neither seemed upset about it.

In a plush chair by the window, a matronly woman with a brooch at her neck knitted what Stella assumed was a scarf, though the shaping seemed like it would be too wide for such a thing. A shawl, perhaps? Whatever it was, she was glad she wasn't the recipient of such a gift since the color of the wool the woman used looked yellow and lumpy like curdled milk.

She and Jeanette commandeered one of the smaller tables. Jeanette watched out the window, so Stella left her maid to her thoughts. Taking advantage of her mother being nowhere near them, she pulled out a Women's Social and Political Union—WSPU—pamphlet and began reading. Her mother would throw a fit if she saw it, so it had stayed folded in Stella's purse since she found it.

"Miss?" She didn't look up. Jeanette sighed and tried again. "Stella?"

When they were younger, when Jeanette had first become her maid, the girl frequently used her name. They were like friends at the time. But age and bitter awareness that they were employer and employee changed their relationship so much that those days were nearly forgotten. For Jeanette to use her name now showed how worried she was.

Stella lowered the pamphlet. "What is it?"

"I hope you don't think me too forward for this"—the girl fidgeted nervously—"but I was wondering if you are marrying Lord Pemberton for the right reasons."

Her mouth went dry at that. "Right reasons?"

Jeanette shifted in her seat. "I apologize, miss. I know it's not my place to question, only you seem so unhappy, and I've worked for you for as long as I've worked, so I feel like I know you better than anyone—"

She was rambling now. Stella held up a hand. The girl cut herself and her long-winded speech off.

"You've only ever had my best interest in mind." Jeanette nodded. Stella set the pamphlet on the table and sighed softly. She glanced towards the doorway to make sure her mother wasn't there. Satisfied, she turned back to Jeanette.

"Lord Pemberton needs my money, but I think he might also need me. We have a chance to be friends, he and I. I think he's more lonely than he lets on."

He didn't stand a chance to save his estate without her. Any simpering girl would bow to the Earl and bend over backwards to please the Dowager Countess. Lord Pemberton needed support in his campaign against them and their traditions. She could be that support.

The maid nodded empathetically. "I think I understand."

But Stella wasn't sure she did. The words tumbled out her mouth desperately. "He has a lot of pressure to maintain his legacy. And I want to help him. I want to stand beside him."

But even as she spoke, it felt like she was trying to convince herself more than Jeanette.

"I understand, miss." There was something in the way Jeanette smiled this time that felt like she was staring into her soul and knew something about Stella that even Stella didn't know.

The train lunged. The brakes squealed as they pulled closer to the station. "We should find my mother."

Jeanette bowed her head and followed after her.

Her mother sat unconcerned in the compartment that she was inhabiting, eyes closed as if she really was sleeping. Stella knew better.

"Mother," she said softly like she would if she was actually trying to wake her. "We're approaching the station."

Her mother startled, much too sudden to be realistic. She reminded Stella of an overdramatic actress. Her mother would loathe that comparison. But she kept quiet and allowed the woman to blink and look up at her.

"Yes, very good."

It was practically a dismissal. Was Stella some sort of servant and not a viscountess-to-be? It took everything in her not to turn and storm from the compartment. She didn't want to give her mother the upper hand.

Among the greeters and well-wishers, Stella spotted a familiar figure standing on the platform talking to another man in a green coat. Her heart throbbed painfully in her chest. It had only been a few days since she saw him last, and she didn't realize she missed him until that moment.

The man looked vaguely familiar, perhaps one of the tenants he had introduced her to? The man removed his hat as he saw her. Mr. Townsend.

Lord Pemberton turned to see who Mr. Townsend was looking at, and a smile slid over his face as he saw her. It was almost like he couldn't help it, his emotions unguarded for a moment. She hadn't seen him look at her that way very often since coming to Wraughtley.

She climbed down and made her way towards him. Despite the disaster in London, her day felt a little bit brighter.

"Mrs. Craven, Miss Craven," Lord Pemberton greeted. Mr. Townsend bowed his head. "I hope it is alright that I brought our driver to bring you back to the house."

"Thank you, Lord Pemberton," her mother said grandly. "That was very thoughtful of you."

The young lord inclined his head. "If you'll excuse me, Mr. Townsend, I can come by later to finish discussing this."

"Of course, my lord. Welcome back, Miss Craven."

"Thank you, Mr. Townsend," she said softly. The other man bowed his head before he turned and walked away.

She liked Mr. Townsend. There was just something about him that seemed to encompass the feeling she got being in Wraughtley. Not around the Earl and his mother, of course, but being around the rest of the village. She had never been one for the countryside and had always wanted more... more excitement, more stores, more people. But the people here were so welcoming, and when Lord Pemberton showed her the lands that would one day be his—theirs—she felt like she could actually make a difference. Like what she said and did would actually matter. It was intoxicating.

Lord Pemberton drew her attention back to him as he led them to the car. "Did you have a pleasant trip?"

"Oh, it was wonderful."

Stella fought the urge to roll her eyes at her mother's theatrics.

ONLY A FEW DAYS after their trip to London, Stella felt like she was being suffocated by the remaining wedding preparations. Not that she was actually allowed to participate in the planning. Most of that stayed between her mother, the Countess, and the Dowager Countess. She was supposed to sit there like she was an ornament, smiling and looking pretty and not giving an opinion.

And so, that afternoon, she decided the only sensible thing that she could do was to sneak out of Pemberton House and into the village. At least there, she wouldn't be forced to smile at another awful flower arrangement. She miscalculated one thing, though. She hadn't expected her mother or the Dowager Countess to be in the parlor.

"Stella dear," she heard her mother call. "Is that you?"

Stella winced. "Yes, Mother."

She shuffled into the doorway, and her mother waved her over.

"Come join us a minute."

She grimaced as her mother turned around but tried to school her expressions before the Dowager Countess spotted it. That would be too much like fresh blood in the water. She took a breath and walked into the room.

Tea sat on the table between the Dowager Countess and her mother. A third chair sat empty, but Stella didn't dare sit. If she did, there would be no escape.

"Yes, Mother?"

The Dowager Countess glared up at her, her mouth set in a straight line. If she hadn't given Stella that look so often, she would be surprised anyone could draw their mouth in such a way.

"Where are you going in such a rush?" her mother asked.

Stella shrugged, attempting to look casual. "I just hoped to get a bit of fresh air."

"In this weather? You won't join us for tea instead?"

Stella glanced back at the door.

"Clearly no," the Dowager Countess said grandly. "She wants to sneak out of the house like a thief in the night."

She glanced down at the chair. It was hardly the first time they talked about her like she wasn't right in front of them. Each time it felt more condescending.

"Oh, I'm sure she didn't mean to—"

"She meant it. She better straighten herself out. She'll hardly be a proper viscountess if she doesn't."

"I agree, no."

Stella swallowed hard. She wouldn't lash out or cry in front of them. She would keep a hold of her emotions.

"Well, go already, girl," the Dowager Countess said. Stella bit her tongue to keep from answering. Her teeth dug sharply into the soft muscle until she drew blood. "Get out of here."

With that, Stella turned and moved from the room as fast as she could without running. She needed to get out of there. She didn't care where.

"Gah!" Furious tears made their way down her cheeks, and she brushed them away. "The nerve of that woman!"

Stella turned into the little garden area that was near the outskirts of the village. Most of the leaves were gone with the end of autumn, and the flowers no longer bloomed. Snow had yet to fall, so the hedges and bushes mostly stood bare. Lord Pemberton admitted that the garden was his pet project, to bring something of beauty into the village before he found out about the depleted coffers.

She dropped onto the stone bench at the center of the hedges with as much grace as she could, closing her eyes to try to block out the world for just a moment. She wanted to be alone, to figure out a way to make the wedding her own, to mend her relationship with Lord Pemberton. While it wasn't as strained since the day she rode to the hill overlooking the village with him, it was not back to the way it had been before she proposed to him.

A chill sunk into her bones. She shivered.

That was when a voice softly called, "Stella?"

No, no, no.

She knew that voice. She hoped to never hear that voice again nor to ever see the face that it belonged to. She didn't want anything to do with him. She didn't want to be around him.

Before her, in all his glory, stood Calvin Wright. He was dressed like a gentleman, with his cane and hat, but there was nothing gentle about him.

"Cal," she greeted, even as she fought the acid bubbling into her throat. "What are you doing here?"

He sat on the bench beside her, and she resisted the urge to move away from him. She wouldn't let him see how much he affected her. That would be like letting him win.

"When I didn't hear from you, and you weren't in Southampton, I went to your hotel in London. They didn't have a forwarding address for you. I had sent you letters, but I suppose you never received them." Stella kept quiet. For a brief second, she wondered if Jeanette had gotten rid of the letters like she had asked in her state of hurt and resentment all of those months ago. "I tried asking your father for a new address."

He grimaced. She could picture how that conversation had gone. Her mother had always hated Cal, and as time went by, Mother seemed to have Father convinced that he was up to no good.

"I'm working for Laverne, um, Miss Castle, my fiancée's father," Cal continued. "His firm sent me to the London office on business. I thought that since I was here, I might try to look for you again before I went back. To see if you were all right. And then, I saw the newspaper announcement about your wedding. It still took me ages to find out where you were." He sounded so honestly confused she almost felt like she should have pity on him. "Did something happen in July?"

"I suppose congratulations are in order." His brow furrowed. "I know about Miss Castle." She stood up to walk away before she turned and snapped, "I was so foolish waiting for you. Telling everyone that we were engaged."

She laughed, but it was a bitter sound. He reached for her.

"Stella, please don't be like that. Sit down. Let's discuss things."

His hand tugged on her wrist until she sat down again. He knew she would be unwilling to cause too much of a scene in public.

"If that's the reason why you agreed to marry this Lord Pemberley—"

"Pemberton," she corrected, hating how small and childish he made her feel. How had she never seen it before?

But Cal continued on like she had never spoken. "Then we can easily get you out of this arrangement. I know you're only marrying him because your mother's forcing you."

"I'm marrying him because I love him!"

Horror set in as her words registered. She recoiled as Cal's hand fell back into his own lap. She took advantage of his shock and collected herself.

"Go home to your fiancée, Cal, and leave me to mine."

With that, she stood up and walked away. She was tempted to take one look back to see if she managed to shock him, but she didn't want to give him power. She didn't want to give him control again. She was starting a new life, and it wasn't right to look back at what she left behind.

IT WAS strange to think that in less than a week, she would be living in Wraughtley Hall. Stella had grown accustomed to the rosy wallpaper and the honey-colored furniture that filled her temporary bedroom in Pemberton House. She wondered if she would be allowed to decorate or have any say in what her room looked like at Wraughtley Hall.

For the first time in weeks, a wave of nostalgia overcame her. She would never see her bedroom in Chicago again—the furniture she had picked out, the linens she had painstakingly selected to match the wallpaper. The clothes she left behind would be packed up and shipped across the ocean.

At the foot of the bed, the wardrobe trunk that she bought in Paris to store most of her trousseau sat wide open. New dresses and blouses fit for her honeymoon, and the early days of marriage hung on the right side while flouncy petticoats peeked out of the drawers. On the bed, ivory silk stockings embroidered with true lover's knots set her face on fire, but those were nothing compared to the lacy negligee and peignoir beside them, meant for her wedding night. Seeing them set her heart pounding loudly in her ears. She swallowed, but her mouth was strangely dry.

She jerked away as the doorknob turned, and she moved quickly to the window and tried her best to act casual and not like she was doing something she shouldn't. It was ridiculous that she felt that way. She was nearly a married woman. There was absolutely nothing wrong with looking at a nightgown, even if it was made of nearly translucent silk.

Jeanette entered, carrying more of her clothes. No, one item of clothing. That horrid wedding dress. That thing was an affront to her sense of fashion—she felt physically ill looking at it—and if her parents hadn't spent so much money on it, she would have burned it.

"Jeanette?" she said so softly that it might have been a whisper. The girl paused her work.

"Yes, miss?"

"I—"

The bed creaked under the weight of the dress. "Miss?"

For a second, it felt like the lacing on her corset was too tight, and she couldn't properly breathe. A half-sob worked its way out of her mouth before she could speak. "Cal showed up in the park while I was on my walk."

"Mr. Wright?" Her voice was as confused as Stella felt. "But I thought…"

Jeanette didn't need to finish. There were too many ways her words could end. Thought that Cal was in America. Thought that he was with Miss Castle. Thought that he didn't care. His appearance should have confused her, but strangely, she felt reassured that she made the right choice asking Lord Pemberton to give her a second chance.

"As did I. Apparently, I am only marrying Lord Pemberton out of desperation. According to Cal–Mr. Wright, anyways."

A tentative hand fell onto her shoulder, patting in what Jeanette probably thought was a comforting gesture. It only helped make her feel like a small child. "Oh, Miss, that's an awful thing to say."

"Isn't it?" She laughed bitterly. "And do you know what I told him? I told him that I was marrying William because I love him."

Jeanette's hand fell away.

"The worst part is," Stella continued like she had never stopped, "that I didn't even realize it was true until after I said it aloud."

And she felt like a fool for using those words as a weapon against someone who shouldn't have been worth her time.

"Have you told him? Lord Pemberton, I mean?"

Stella shook her head and collapsed in the chair by the window. Her legs were unable to support her any longer as the world seemed to slide from under her feet. She blinked back tears.

That was probably the first time she had referred to him as

William. The first time she even thought of him as anything other than 'Lord Pemberton.' She tried for so long to keep him at arm's length that she hadn't even realized…

"It doesn't matter," she whispered weakly. "It doesn't change anything."

"Miss…"

She looked up, steeling herself. "No, Jeanette. This is just a business arrangement. I've accepted that. There's no use in worrying over things that can't be changed."

Jeanette swallowed hard. "Yes, miss."

The girl moved back towards the bed and shook out the stockings and the negligee.

Stella glanced out the window, watching the late-afternoon sky as the sun sunk behind the tops of the trees. She felt like an idiot. Nothing Jeanette could say would change that. She spent all this time acting like she was some sort of victim, and she wasn't. It was her choice to marry William. Cal had offered her a way out, and she rejected it, which meant she would rather be here. Whatever happened next, she would rather face it by William's side.

Jeanette lifted that atrocious nightmare, and Stella knew with utter certainty that she could not wear that dress. She couldn't even entertain the notion of wearing it any longer. Not with mere days left before the wedding.

"I need your help with something," she said suddenly, "and I need you to keep it a secret."

Jeanette dropped the dress in surprise, pivoting to look at Stella. Her brow scrunched up. The corners of her lips turned. down slightly. "Of course, miss. Anything."

Things would work out in the end. Stella knew they would.

19

———

WILLIAM

IN THE TIME since Stella and Mrs. Craven returned from London, William barely saw either of them with the exception of an occasional dinner at Wraughtley Hall. He hoped that he and Stella had come to better terms again, but it was foolish to think that she would have any time with the last-minute wedding preparations to actually see him.

Which was horrible because he found he wanted to see her desperately. The wedding was tomorrow, and he wasn't supposed to see her until she walked in the doors of the church, but he felt like he was seeing her everywhere. That was the only reason why he even noticed when her maid walked briskly across the street in front of him. He had only seen her a handful of times, and he probably wouldn't have remembered her if she didn't look so much like his fiancée.

"Hello," he said to her. "Aren't you Miss Craven's maid?"

She squeaked, the noise high-pitched and sounding rather like a mouse. She dropped into a low curtsy, stuttering as she spoke, "L-L-Lord P-P-Pemberton."

"Are you alright?"

She bobbed her head several times. "Yes, my lord."

He would have thought that he had caught her doing something highly illegal with as nervous as she was acting. A thought struck him suddenly. "Is everything alright with Miss Craven?"

He knew they were close.

"Of course, my lord."

He barely contained his breath of relief. For a second, he wondered if she regretted this and decided to call the wedding off, and he was the last to know.

"If that's everything, my lord, I really need to be going."

He nodded. "Of course. I didn't mean to hold you up."

She dipped into a curtsy again before she turned, all but running into one of the nearby shops. The dress store? Sometimes, Margaret shopped there. She usually claimed that buying clothes locally was good for the village and good for morale. The latest reason, though, was because Margaret visited her kitten daily.

The village was decorated for Christmas. Wreaths hung in every doorway, and festive strings of garland lined the windows. A Christmas wedding seemed like the perfect time for new beginnings.

"Lord Pemberley?"

William almost ignored the man that spoke. It wasn't his name. It always annoyed him when people got it wrong.

The man spoke with an American accent, which threw him off a little. He didn't think any of Stella's relatives who traveled there for the wedding would mispronounce his name.

"Pemberton," he corrected as he turned.

The man in front of him was younger than Stella's brother and far too young to be her father. He didn't recall any other male relatives of hers who would be attending the wedding. The man was good-looking too, the kind of man Margaret usually swooned over.

"And you are?"

"Calvin Wright." The man offered a hand. William eyed it distastefully, but he shook it.

Was this really the man Stella had claimed she was going to marry?

"What can I do for you, Mr. Wright?"

"Actually, it's what I can do for you. Can we talk somewhere more private?"

William bowed his head, acquiescing with the other man's request if only to keep them from coming to blows in the middle of the street. The man's smug expression made William's fingers twitch and ball his hands into fists.

Why was he here? Did Stella ask him? Did he come to win her back or to convince her not to go through with the wedding?

The last thought made his throat tighten. He didn't want her to leave. He'd grown accustomed to seeing her, to walking through the village with her, to making eye contact across the table, and spending time together even if she was holding back. The idea of that ending now was unbearable.

He followed Wright to the public gardens near the edge of the village. Was this really the other man's idea of a private place, or was this just the only place in town that he knew? William would have bet his money on the latter.

"I should have left," the other man started. "She told me to, but I didn't want to leave things the way we did."

It didn't take a genius to realize he was talking about Stella.

Wright shook his head. "I know she doesn't want to talk to me, but she's one of my oldest friends. I'm sorry about what I said, I'm sorry to have hurt her, and I want to do one thing for her before I leave."

William couldn't help but stare at him. What did any of that have to do with him, he wondered. His brow furrowed, but he didn't say anything, allowing the other man to continue.

"She loves you."

His mind blanked for a moment before the words registered in his head. William knew better than to disagree with him, even if he knew the other man was wrong. Something on his face must have said it as clearly as if he had spoken aloud.

"She does," the man insisted. "She told me so."

"Why did she tell you?" he asked, trying desperately to keep the notes of anger and defensiveness out of his voice. Why would she tell this man something so personal and not him?

"We were arguing." That wasn't a surprise. She hadn't mentioned Calvin Wright once since they'd been in Wraughtley. It was almost taboo. The few times he had tea with his grandmother and Stella and her mother, Mrs. Craven avoided the topic completely. "I think she was more surprised than I was when she blurted it out."

Blurted it out? It was a little depressing that she had told this man before him, but at the same time, the impulsiveness of the action sounded like Stella.

She loved him.

Stella loved him. The thought made him feel warm inside. All this time, he thought she was going through with this marriage out of some desire for revenge on Wright or to spite her mother, though he wasn't entirely sure how doing as her mother wanted worked to spite her.

But did she really love him? Or was that just something that Wright said, trying to get into his head? Or perhaps Stella had said it in hopes of evoking some sort of reaction from Wright.

William swallowed hard and tried to keep any trace of emotion from showing on his face.

"You could always ask her if you don't believe me. I knew she probably hadn't said anything and likely wouldn't, considering she's as stubborn as a mule, but I thought you should know." Wright bowed his head. "I wish we could have met under more pleasant circumstances."

He offered his hand again. This time, William took it without hesitation.

"Have a safe journey."

"Thank you. And congratulations. I hope the two of you will be very happy together."

With that, Wright walked away. Perhaps the strangest part of the conversation to William was the fact that the man sounded like he meant all of it.

He shook his head. He needed to see Stella. It couldn't wait until tomorrow.

20

____

STELLA

IT WAS ONLY two weeks ago that her father, brother, and sister had arrived in Pemberton. They were staying at Pemberton House, and, as a result, the house felt overcrowded, bordering on claustrophobic at times. Since they arrived, Stella hadn't had a moment to herself.

Stella escaped out of Pemberton House, her feet carrying her down to the Dowager Countess' garden. She needed to be away from everyone. The house was too stuffy, and no one wanted to give her any space. It was like her mother thought Stella might run off if she was alone for a second.

In the brisk winter air, it was easier to breathe.

She hoped Jeanette managed to slip back in the house without her mother or Dowager Countess seeing her. Stella didn't want to ruin the surprise before she walked into the church tomorrow. It would give them too much time to change things if anyone but Jeanette saw her before the ceremony.

It was strange to think by that time tomorrow, she would be a married woman. Her mother would no longer be able to control her, and her future mother-in-law seemed like a reasonable woman.

Cal got in her head. She hated that he still had any power over her. Ever since he'd pulled her confession from her, her heart hadn't stopped throbbing.

A lone figure wandered down the path from the house. Her breath caught in her throat. William…

What on earth is he doing here?

William walked towards her. His head turned side to side as if he was scanning the grounds. He paused as he saw her before he came closer. His steps were hesitant. Would he leave before he talked to her?

"It's bad luck to see the bride before the wedding," she called to him while he was still far enough away to turn back. The odd expression on his face made her shudder. She wanted to tell herself that her curiosity was the only thing that made her walk closer.

The wedding wasn't until tomorrow, but her mother and the Dowager Countess were both superstitious. She doubted they were the ones to tell him where she was.

"I ran into an interesting character earlier."

Her heart stuttered. Interesting character… surely Calvin hadn't stuck around? He had no reason to.

"Oh?" she asked, attempting to play coy. She knew, somehow, that it had to be Cal. The way William was looking at her, it couldn't have been anyone else.

He reached out to her and offered his hand. Reluctantly, she took it and held it tightly. If she let go, she might lose him forever, and that was the last thing she wanted. He led her further into the gardens, into the tall, sturdy hedges.

What had Cal said to him?

There was a little bench in the garden. It was white and made out of wires twisted together into intricate designs. He led them to it, and they sat. Her nerves ate at her stomach. What would he say? Did Cal say something to upset him? His expression was certainly unreadable enough.

"I met your Mr. Wright," William said softly.

Stella swallowed and glanced down at the bench. It was interesting enough to look at. The wires formed some sort of mesh, crisscrossing over each other and looping around the frame. His hand reached out to her, touching her cheek softly, and she looked up.

"He was surprisingly cordial, other than the fact that he couldn't remember my name."

She cringed. "What did he say?"

"He was sorry to have hurt you." His fingers ran down her cheek, his touch so gentle that she could have cried. She looked up into his eyes and knew Cal had told him what she said. She swallowed again, her mouth suddenly very dry.

"I'm sorry," she whispered. Her words felt stuck in her throat. "I haven't been very fair to you. I've been selfish." His hand stilled on her cheek. "I've kept you at arm's length."

"Why have you?" He wasn't accusing, just curious. He didn't look angry.

"I've been afraid," she admitted, feeling a bit foolish about it. She didn't want to be hurt again. In the process, all she had done was torture both of them. She should have known better. "I think it's time for me to be brave."

His hand slid to cup her face. "Maybe I should have been braver too."

With that, he leaned in and pressed his lips to hers. It wasn't earth-shattering. The world didn't stop spinning around them. No winged cherubs played harps as they floated around them. But it felt right.

STELLA WALKED BACK UPSTAIRS as the sun faded from the sky as she did her best to avoid everyone. She was floating. Stella hoped her mother stayed away until dinner. She didn't want anything to ruin that moment. When was the last time she was that happy? For the first time, she didn't dread tomorrow.

Someone rapped quickly at the door as if they were afraid to be overheard. She stood and unlocked the door, and Jeanette rushed in.

"Hurry," she commanded. Jeanette carried a large package wrapped in tissue paper and tied up in a string. It was inconspicuous, other than the fact that she had brought it upstairs. Stella locked the door behind her. "Is that it?"

Jeanette nodded and set the package on the bed. She pulled the strings and revealed the cannibalized dress in its wrappings. Carefully, Jeanette helped her lift it up so Stella could see the finished product. When she sent her maid to the dressmakers with the gown, she wasn't entirely sure what to expect.

Her breath caught in her throat.

It barely resembled the dress she first wore when she met William. The original green underdress had been ripped from the white lace and replaced with a much softer ivory. Beading made the dress shimmer as it moved through the light. The original belt that matched the underdress had been replaced by white satin, wrapped around the waist to keep the silhouette the same. It didn't have a long, heavy train like the gown her mother had chosen. Instead, Miss Carr and Miss Austin somehow managed to find a near-identical piece of lace that they added to the bottom of the dress to create a long but much less beaded train.

In theory, Stella could have just used the gown she had worn for her court presentation. It was white and elaborate, but it was more suited to her mother's tastes than Stella's.

No. This dress was perfect.

21

———

WILLIAM

WILLIAM HAD NEVER BEEN MORE nervous in his life. It didn't make any sense. What was there left to be nervous about? And yet, everything in him felt like it was vibrating, waiting for something to go wrong.

He walked into the church he attended all his life and hoped his hands didn't shake too much. Every seat was filled. The entire county seemed to have come out for the event, along with several friends of the family who had travelled from across England to be there. Servants from the house and the villagers filled the back pews. The more important guests were in the front.

Bertie stayed by his side; William assumed to make sure he didn't run away. But why would he run?

Last night, Stella told him she loved him, and he had whispered the words back. They spent hours together until the light disappeared, and he sent her back before anyone realized she was missing. The secret, forbidden kiss. His grandmother would have died if she knew that he had been alone with Stella, unchaperoned at her house before the wedding. Just thinking about it brought blood rushing to his cheeks.

Mrs. Craven appeared to have just arrived moments before him. Her dress was covered in frilly lace, and he was struck once again by the dissimilarities between her and her daughter.

Stella would have been horrified by such an ensemble. Her tastes ran towards the modern styles that he found he was rather fond of, but her mother wore the ruffled outfit proudly.

Stella's brother waited in the pew for his mother. *Her brother's name was Ambrose,* his mind supplied helpfully, remembering Stella's introduction to the man who taught her how to drive. He wasn't entirely sure if he liked Ambrose or not, but since Stella made an effort to get to know Margaret, he could surely do the same with her siblings.

Beside Mrs. Craven sat the rest of Stella's family. Mr. Craven's sister had married an earl, now deceased. She wore a deep, dark purple gown that wasn't nearly as stiff as her sister-in-law's. Her son was the new Earl of Astermore. Next to the earl's wife was the earl's sister, Lady Theodora, who looked like she would rather be anywhere else but there. William had met so many people in the last few days, and he never expected that Stella had so many relatives in England.

Euphemia Craven, the tiny spitfire that reminded him so much of her older sister, walked briskly down to their pew. She wore something that looked like she borrowed it from Stella. The dress she wore bordered on risqué, and he was surprised that she chose to wear something so tightly fitted in a church.

"Mother," he heard the girl ask, "have you seen Stella?"

He tensed. He knew her sister had been at Pemberton House aiding Stella in getting ready, but he thought her mother had also been.

"Of course I have. I watched her get into the carriage."

The carriage would circle through Pemberton and go up to the Wraughtley Hall so that anyone who had been unable to get away for the ceremony could still see the bridal carriage before coming back towards the church. So Stella was already on her way. He let out a sigh of relief. Not that he thought she would back out now, but part of him couldn't help the dread bubbling at the back of his mind.

"Her dress! She looks so pretty!"

Mrs. Craven scoffed and puffed up in a fair impersonation of a peacock fanning out his tail. "I picked it out. I knew she would like it."

"You did?" Something in the girl's tone made him pause. Disbelief? What was Stella planning? She had to be up to something; otherwise, why would her sister be confused about her dress?

He sat down in the front pew beside Bertie. Someone would let him know when to stand. He lifted his hand from his lap and watched as it trembled. He pulled out his pocket watch and clicked the cover open and shut several times. The weight felt good in his hands. Solid.

"Nervous?" his friend asked, lifting his brows knowingly.

"No." He clenched his hand tightly. It wasn't so much nerves at this point. More like anxiety. The tension that came with waiting. The anticipation of what was to come.

He flipped the cover open again and glanced down at the time. A knot tightened in his chest and throat until he felt like he couldn't properly swallow.

Stella was running late. What if she had changed her mind? She could have decided that this was all a bad idea. Wright was probably still waiting somewhere in the shadows, ready to spirit her away.

"Do you think he's going to be alright?" Euphemia hissed. Her voice carried over the dull murmurs in the church. Somehow, he knew she was staring at him. It felt like her eyes were boring holes into his neck.

"Euphemia, darling"—Mrs. Craven's voice came next— "please sit down and stop asking ridiculous questions."

There was a quiet, "Yes, Mother," before there was silence from that side of the aisle.

Outside, the bells clanged loudly, and people cheered. His heart raced faster as the music started. He shoved the watch in his pocket. Bertie grinned and patted him on the shoulder.

"Good luck."

"Thank you," he whispered, stepping up to the front of the church. The priest, Father Storey, gave him a reassuring smile. The same man who had seen him baptized would see him married. It hadn't seemed like such a big deal until that moment.

William fought the urge to turn around to watch Stella come down the aisle. He heard the audience stand, and William closed his eyes, focusing on the music. Shoes clacked softly on the stone floor directly behind him.

At that moment, he heard the gasps and could no longer resist the urge to look.

His breath caught in his throat as he saw Stella, her hand in the crook of her father's arm. She was stunning, gorgeous, like a figure that stepped out of his dreams.

The ethereal figure moved towards him. On her head, a shimmer of diamonds caught the light and sparkled like a halo, even beneath the veil.

As she got closer, he recognized the tiara she wore as his mother's. It was one of her favorites... she had worn it on birthdays and anniversaries for as long as he could remember.

Stella's eyes lifted from the ground, from the spot that she had been staring, and met his. A grin spread across her face.

The knot in his chest relaxed, and he could breathe again.

As Stella passed, out of the corner of his eye, he could see her sister beaming.

"Doesn't she look lovely?" he could hear her sister say.

"That's not the dress," her mother muttered from her place

in the front row, as Mrs. Craven stared at her daughter, eyes wide.

His eyes flickered down. To be honest, he hadn't paid attention to what she wore, besides the fact that she looked radiant. It seemed a fair bit simpler than anything Mrs. Craven wore.

Oh, he thought dumbly as it hit him. *That's why she had been running late. She had switched dresses.*

They stopped at the end of the aisle. Mr. Craven stepped away as Stella took her place beside him. She glanced up at him. He smiled at her, his early panic forgotten.

He dropped his voice to a whisper and hoped no one would hear him over the music. "You are magnificent."

Her smile lifted at the corners.

"I hope you don't mind that I was running a bit late," she murmured back in the same soft tone. She shifted the flowers in her hand. "I came to the realization that this was our wedding and not my mother's or your grandmother's."

"Hence the dress."

She giggled, the sound so uncharacteristic that it took everything in him not to jerk his head in her direction. "Hence the dress."

The music died down. People shuffled behind them as they sat down, and Father Storey cleared his throat. "Dearly beloved, we are gathered here today to join this man and this woman in holy matrimony."

William let out a breath.

FOUR YEARS LATER
STELLA

THE GARDENS at Wraughtley Hall were always lovely in the spring, just after the snow melted and the plants recovered from winter. This would be their last walk in the gardens before they left for London. Spring was always Stella's favorite time to be there before she and her husband traveled back to London for the Season. London meant balls and races, and while she had always loved those things, now they just made her feel sad. It had been almost four years since that day in Hyde Park, and nothing had changed for women. Stella wasn't able to make anything change for women.

Instead, she had refocused to where she could do the most good. She once told Jeanette that William needed her and needed her money. In the months after the wedding, that was more true than she could have ever predicted.

The old Earl died while they were on their honeymoon. He fell from his horse and had broken his neck. William had been torn between being devastated at the loss of his father and relieved that he was finally free to do what he thought was best for the family. But those thoughts made him feel guilty, and he needed her to help him, support him, and keep him sane in the months that followed. If she hadn't been there, there were days she doubted he would have left the study or gone to bed.

After returning from their honeymoon and after her and William settled into their new roles, Stella had written to Cal to apologize for her behavior. Knowing her as well as he did, Cal teased her in his return letter about her temper, but invited her and William to come to his wedding to Miss Castle the following spring, and they resumed their correspondence.

"Are you happy?" William asked, his voice practically a caress against her ear. She shuddered, his breath warm against her skin. He asked from time to time as if he still couldn't believe they were together.

She leaned forward and pressed her lips to the corner of his mouth, even as she kept her hands to herself. His head tilted, turning slightly to deepen the kiss, but she pulled back before he could. He groaned in frustration, and Stella smirked. "I am."

He glared slightly. His head dropped until his forehead met hers. She laughed. Her fingers reached up and twisted into his hair as her eyes studied him. If this was the last bit of time they would be alone for a while, it was the perfect time to tell him that—

"Mama!" a sharp, shrill little voice cried out. "Papa!"

At three, their daughter Imogen had the most impressive set of lungs Stella ever encountered. Her shouting was all the more warning they received before she collided with their legs.

"Papa! Up!" Imogen seemed to somehow mistake William's trouser leg with Stella's dress and tugged at it until her father paid her the proper amount of attention.

William snorted and pulled away from Stella as he lifted the girl. Her play clothes were rumpled, and her ringlets hung loosely around her shoulders. "Hello, love. What brings you out here?"

He glanced at Stella, his expression clearly amused.

"Papa!" the girl said again as if she hadn't already. "Aunt Maggie wants me to throw flowers!"

Stella laughed. So Margaret had arrived.

"Does she now?" William asked in a tone that actually sounded like he was interested. Their daughter nodded enthusiastically before she continued telling her father all about the flowers and something about Bertie in garbled sentences. By the end of her tale, Stella had come to the conclusion that Margaret and Bertie were now engaged.

The nurse they hired to watch their daughter—a usually put-together woman aptly named Patience—chased after Imogen, looking rather harried and frazzled as she did so. Her eyes went wide as she saw the child in William's arms, and she barely stopped in front of them before she let out a sigh of relief.

"I'm so sorry, my lord, my lady. She got away from me."

"Oh, that's alright. Imogen had some important news to tell us. Didn't you, darling?"

Imogen nodded, hiding her head shyly into her father's shoulder. Apparently, now that her news had been told, she no longer wanted to be the center of attention.

"So you're going to be a flower girl in your Aunt Margaret's wedding?" Stella rubbed her stomach absentmindedly, pausing her actions as she realized just what she was doing.

"Uh-huh. And wear a pretty dress. And throw flowers." It seemed that the most important part of being a flower girl to her was the fact that she got to throw things, and the adults would allow her.

"I'm sure your great-granny will have a thing or two to say about that."

William's grandmother would certainly have a fit. He laughed and pressed a quick kiss to Stella's cheek. Imogen scrunched her nose and turned her head away. William smiled at them.

"She always does."

LADY THEA'S WORLD

Lady Theodora has her own series of adventures in her historical cozy mystery series set 1910, two years after the main events in *An Invitation to Tea*.

~

Murder on the Flying Scotsman

As the 1910 London Season comes to an end, it's time for Lady Theodora Prescott-Pryce's annual pilgrimage to visit her cousins in Scotland. Accompanied by only her maid, Molly, she thinks she's in for another long, dull trip aboard the Flying Scotsman.

The last thing she expects to find as they departed from London is a body in her compartment. Despite Molly being accused of the murder, Thea knows her maid is innocent.

Aided by a young Scotland Yard inspector and an American heiress, Thea uses the detective skills she learned from reading Sherlock Holmes to track down the real murderer, but will she find them before they can strike again?

<u>Lady Thea Mystery</u>

Book 1: Murder on the Flying Scotsman

Book 1.5: The Unread Letter

Book 2: The Corpse at Ravenholm Castle

Book 3: A Most Fashionable Murder

Book 3.5: A Christmas Puzzle

An Invitation to Tea: A Historical Romance Novella

ACKNOWLEDGMENTS

Thank you so much to:
Bethany, Shanté, Megan, Lynn, Jerri, and my parents.

For all of your help and support on this book.
Without you, this story would not be what it is.

ABOUT THE AUTHOR

Named for the famous fictional mystery writer Jessica Fletcher, Jessica Baker picked up a pen when she was in elementary school and never set it down.

Jessica lives in sunny Central Florida and is a member of the Sisters in Crime. When she's not writing, she works at a university and freelances as a camera assistant in film which provides plenty of inspiration for her stories.

To learn more about Jessica and her books, visit her at www.jessicabakerauthor.com and for the latest information, subscribe to her newsletters.

www.ingramcontent.com/pod-product-compliance
Lightning Source LLC
Chambersburg PA
CBHW030205130726
47898CB00012B/883